Melissa's grip tightened on Jonathan's arm.

He looked down at her, her face pale to the lips, her eyes wide. "Oh no," she moaned.

"My wife and I"—Almina had joined Lawrence Brooke, tucking her arm into his elbow and beaming on the crowd, her gaze lingering longest on Jonathan and Melissa—"are pleased to announce the engagement of our daughter, Melissa, to Mr. Jonathan Kennebrae. Please join us in congratulating the happy couple." He lifted the glass in their direction.

A polite wave of applause welled up.

Melissa stood, knocking her chair over onto the grass. She put her hand to her mouth, turning her head wildly from Jonathan to her parents then back again.

Jonathan rose slowly, easing up on numb legs.

"Kennebrae?" She whispered so low he had to stoop to hear her. "Your name is Kennebrae?"

"Of course it is. What else would it be?"

She blinked, staring at him. "But I thought—" Her throat spasmed as she tried to swallow. "I thought. . ."

He caught her just before she hit the grass in a dead faint.

ERICA VETSCH is married to Peter and keeps the company books for the family lumber business. A homeschool mom to Heather and James, Erica loves history, romance, and storytelling. Her ideal vacation is taking her family to out-of-the-way history museums and chatting to curators about local history. She has a bachelor's degree from Calvary Bible College in secondary education: social studies. You can find her on the Web at www.onthewritepath.blogspot.com.

The Bartered Bride

Erica Vetsch

Heartsong Presents

For Peter, Heather, and James Vetsch. All my love.

Author Note:
For more information on the *Mataafa*, the historical ship upon which the fictional *Kennebrae Bethany* is based, please visit the Minnesota Historical Society Web site at www.mnhs.org, keyword: Mataafa.

A note from the Author:
I love to hear from my readers! You may correspond with me by writing:

Erica Vetsch
Author Relations
PO Box 721
Uhrichsville, OH 44683

ISBN 978-1-60260-589-3

THE BARTERED BRIDE

All scripture quotations are taken from the King James Version of the Bible.

All of the characters and events in this book are fictitious. Any resemblance to actual persons, living or dead, or to actual events is purely coincidental.

Our mission is to publish and distribute inspirational products offering exceptional value and biblical encouragement to the masses.

PRINTED IN THE U.S.A.

one

"The idea's preposterous, and I'll have nothing to do with it." Jonathan Kennebrae bolted from his chair and stalked across the office. "You won't manipulate me like this. And I doubt Noah or Eli will go along with the scheme either."

His grandfather, Abraham Kennebrae, sat ramrod straight behind the walnut desk. For a man confined to an invalid chair these past eight years, his voice still rang with authority and vigor. "I've spent a lifetime building up this family's fortune and power, and I want to die knowing it will continue. If not through you, then through your brothers. The best way to ensure this is to marry you boys off well. You act as if contracted marriage was something new. It's been going on for centuries."

Jonathan clasped his hands behind his back under his coattails and stared out the window of Grandfather's library. Two acres of emerald grass stretched below to the shoreline. Lake Superior spread before him, cobalt blue under an azure sky. *The Lady Genevieve,* the family yacht named for his grandmother, bobbed gently along the dock beside the boathouse. Her white hull gleamed, her mast pointed to the cloudless heavens. He wished he stood at her wheel, skimming over the waves, away from this incredible conversation.

"It's all arranged, Jonathan. Three weddings, three sound marriages, and the consolidation of four of the wealthiest families in Duluth. And not only that, but it brings together under one name all you need to control every aspect of this harbor: shipping, grain, ore, and lumber."

Jonathan turned and leaned against the windowsill. The morning sun fell through the stained glass of the upper windows, shattering rainbows on the Persian rug. He crossed his ankles, trying to appear casual. "All arranged? You and your cronies have everything mapped out? And Noah, Eli, and I have no say? Have you decided who is to marry whom, or were you just going to have us draw straws?"

His jaw ached, and the pain between his eyebrows increased. An image of Grandfather and his bewhiskered, cigar-smoking circle of friends bending over charts and arguing the relative merits of their offspring wavered before his eyes. "I have no intention of marrying an empty-headed showpiece chosen by you. Are your grandsons no more than pawns to be shuffled about at your command? Whose idea was this?" His throat ached with the desire to yell, but years of training and deference to the man before him kept his voice controlled.

"Now, lad"—Grandfather made a dismissing motion—"you make it sound worse than it is."

"I don't see how that's possible. I feel like a horse at auction. Did you sell us to the highest bidders?" Sarcasm dripped out, laced with exasperation.

Grandfather wagged a gnarled finger. "Don't take that tone with me. I'm still the head of this household. I made a sound business decision for this family. You'll accede to my wishes in this. You're nearly thirty. It's past time you were married and setting up your household. As a member of the aristocracy of this city and this state, you have an obligation to marry well."

"Shades of the Four Hundred." Jonathan jammed his hands into his pockets. "This is 1905, and your ideas are outdated. This isn't New York City. It's Duluth. I'm not marrying someone so I can be invited to better parties and promenade through Newport every afternoon during 'The Season.' And I'm certainly not interested in any female who wishes to marry for those reasons either."

"You couldn't be further from the truth. You aren't marrying into the salons of Fifth Avenue. You're marrying to gain control of the harbor." He waved his hand in a sweeping motion toward the lake. "Control that harbor, and you control millions of dollars. Control millions, and you control the politicians in St. Paul and Washington. Control St. Paul and Washington, and you control the power to make more millions. Don't you see it?"

"What if I don't want to control the harbor? What if I'm content with what I have: a solid business with an excellent reputation and a sound financial base?"

"Then you're a fool. You'll have wasted everything I've spent my life building up. Now is the time to strike. Of the four richest families in Duluth, I'm the only one with male heirs. Lawrence Brooke, Phillip Michaels, and Radcliffe Zahn have only daughters. And don't forget, a marriage to Lawrence Brooke's daughter brings not just the grain docks in the harbor but the railroad that hauls the grain from the Dakotas, too."

Jonathan ran his hand over his hair. "You still haven't convinced me. I don't even know these women. Why would I want to marry any of them?"

Grandfather thumped the blotter. "Stop being obtuse. I'll make it as plain as possible. You will court and marry the daughter of Lawrence Brooke, you will gain control of the grain docks in Duluth harbor, and you will do so before Christmas."

"Before Christmas? That's impossible. Christmas is less than three months away. Isn't that a bit quick?"

"Poppycock. I see no reason to wait. Waiting only increases the chances that something will go wrong. We must act now. You, as the eldest, will set an example for your brothers. The twins will fall in line. And it isn't as if the young women won't receive the benefits of a sound match. Wealth, status, security, influence. What more could a woman want?"

Jonathan snorted. "I'm no expert on the female mind. I have no idea what they want. But what happens if I don't do as you say? Or what if the woman won't have me?"

"I will disinherit you without so much as a blink." Grandfather regarded him with glittering eyes. "I will leave my fortune only to those grandsons who do my bidding. Those who will not, receive nothing. I've already rewritten my will to reflect the changes."

Anger replaced the exasperation and unbelief in Jonathan's chest. "You cannot be serious."

"I've never been more serious in my life." Grandfather narrowed his eyes and pursed his lips, causing his wiry side-whiskers to bristle out like a badger. "Do you care to challenge me? The will stands as long as the girl is legally free and morally acceptable for you to wed."

Jonathan's mind raced, and his muscles tensed. How dare that old reprobate? Kennebrae Shipping was his. He'd run the company, chaired the board, and overseen the day-to-day operations for the past eight years. He, not Grandfather, had expanded the fleet, brokered new contracts, enticed investors. The company was his life. He'd be dead before he'd let anyone take it from him.

A knock sounded on the library door. The butler entered, a silver tray in his hand. "This just arrived for you, sir." He extended the salver toward Grandfather.

The old man took an envelope from it and turned it in his hands.

"Will there be a reply, sir? The gentleman who delivered it is waiting."

Grandfather picked up his letter opener. He slit the heavy cream envelope and read, satisfaction spreading over his face. His fingers drummed the desktop.

Jonathan paced between the marble fireplace and the glass-front bookcases. Grandfather's words were no idle threat. He'd disinherit Jonathan without so much as a by-your-leave should Jonathan cross him. He had seen it in the old man's eyes. Galling, that's what it was. To have a bride chosen for him based upon her wealth and connections. And worse, to be chosen as a husband based on his.

Grandfather leaned forward and uncapped the silver inkwell. He dipped his ebony pen in the liquid and scratched a few words on the card. "McKay, give the gentleman this."

"Very good, sir."

The door had barely closed before Jonathan whirled from contemplating the oil painting over the mantel. "Do Noah and Eli know about this?"

"No, of course not. I'll tell Noah when he returns to the harbor, and I'll tell Eli when he returns from Virginia. Though why Eli can't learn shipbuilding right here in Duluth is beyond me."

"He wanted to learn from the best, and the best shipbuilders are on the East Coast." Jonathan rubbed his palm against the back of his neck. How could he get out of this? His strides measured the room.

"Will you stop pacing like a caged wolf? You'd think I was asking you to go to the gallows." Grandfather backed his chair and wheeled it around the edge of the desk. A blanket covered his stick-thin legs from hips to ankles.

Jonathan sagged onto the horsehair settee. "From what I can tell, marriage and hanging have a lot in common. The man ends up dangling from the end of a string either way."

Grandfather chuckled then shook his head. "Where'd you get an idea like that? Your grandmother, God rest her soul, was a fine woman."

"What about my parents? To hear you talk, they couldn't be in the same room without bloodshed. How they wound up with three sons is beyond me."

Sadness lined Grandfather's face. "Your parents were both high-strung. Always convinced the other was being a fool. But they loved each other, in their own way. I thought they'd settle down eventually. It's a shame you never got to know them. Your father couldn't live without her. The carriage accident was a mercy. He was never the same after your mother died. And neither were you, though you were only four at the time."

"I have no real memories of my parents, only their portraits in the drawing room."

"Those were your grandmother's idea. Had them painted from their engagement pictures. Thought it might be nice for you boys to have them."

Jonathan took note of the nostalgic look in Grandfather's eyes. If he could just keep him talking about old times, about Grandmother, perhaps he would forget this nonsense about marriage.

"She was a saint. And what she ever saw in an old boot like you, I'll never know."

"Hah! That's just what her parents said when I came courting. Never thought I'd amount to anything. But I showed them. Built up the biggest shipping line on the Great Lakes and built Kennebrae House for your grandmother, too. Nothing was too good for her."

"She deserved every one of the fifty-five rooms for putting up with you."

"Well, your new wife will, too."

Jonathan blew out a breath. So much for getting Grandfather off the subject. "I haven't agreed to this madness. Anyway, I think you're assuming a lot. I haven't even met this Miss Brooke. We might not suit one another at all."

"You're both young and rich. You'll suit one another just fine. How do you feel about music?"

"What?"

"I asked how you felt about music. An evening of music and fine food."

What kind of sidetrack was this? Jonathan put his guard firmly up.

The old man had a gleam in his eye, an unholy sparkle that boded no good.

"You mean one of those parties where the hostess shoves her daughter onstage, and the poor girl scrapes away at some writhing violin concerto or pounds out a tortured nocturne on the piano while the audience tries not to wince or die from boredom? And at dinner they make up compliments over dried-out chicken and pasty potatoes until they can make a graceful escape?"

"I hope it isn't as bad as you describe."

"What are you hatching?"

"The note that came earlier. It was an invitation to Castle-brooke. Mrs. Brooke is having an evening of music and re-freshments tonight. I sent the reply that both of us would be delighted to attend. And you'll have ample time to study your bride-to-be. She'll be the one performing the tortured nocturnes."

two

Melissa Brooke stared into her mirror and caught the reflection of her new evening gown hanging on the wardrobe behind her. A couture creation from the House of Worth in Paris, the gown was everything she'd dreamed it would be when she ordered it. Now if only her piano performance lived up to the dress. Should she attempt the Chopin or stay with the Mozart for the opening? Melissa bit the edge of her fingernail.

Sarah, her maid, ran a brush through Melissa's dark brown hair and began the task of pinning the heavy curls up for the evening.

Mother swept into the room. "You'll ruin your manicure, Melissa, if you don't stop that dreadful habit." A tiny woman, Almina Brooke carried herself regally, appearing much taller. She paused before the wardrobe, tweaking the sleeves of Melissa's gown.

Melissa dropped her hand to her lap and made a face at her reflection.

"And stop that scowling. You'll get wrinkles." Mother, in her dressing gown but with her hair already styled, sat on the end of the powder blue chaise longue. "The guests will arrive in a half hour or so. The servants have lit the gas lamps in the music room. I don't think this newfangled electricity burns as brightly. I told your father it was a fad when we built this place. But he wouldn't listen." She smoothed her yellow satin belt. "Are you nervous?"

"A little. How many people did you say would be attending?" Melissa winced as Sarah jerked at a snarl.

"Sorry, miss."

"Only a small soiree, dear—sixty people. Just right for

the music room. Nothing too ostentatious. We want this gathering to be cozy and intimate. That's why you're the only musician tonight. I want you to be the centerpiece."

"You make me sound like a bowl of chrysanthemums." Melissa ignored the tiny wings flapping in her middle. "I think you and I have different ideas as to what constitutes small and intimate. Anyway, I thought this was more of a business evening for Father. He said he had associates attending."

"Actually, that's what I came to talk to you about. Tonight is a big night. Your father has invited two particularly important guests, and I'm counting on you to make a good impression, especially on one of them. Don't frown at me, young lady." She pointed a finger heavy with diamonds at Melissa. "It's time you were making wedding plans. You've had a debut to rival a Vanderbilt's. If we lived in New York, you'd have had the cream of society calling on you, maybe even a titled European or two."

Melissa held hairpins up one at a time for Sarah. "I don't want all that. And I'm not ready to get married yet. I have so much I want to do before I think about marriage."

Mother sniffed down her nose. "Your so-called 'progressive' ideas. What you need is your own household to run and your own husband to look after so you'll forget this nonsense. Your father and I have worked very hard to find a suitable match for you, and you're not going to ruin it. You'll be polite, charming, and keep your radical ideas to yourself. You will impress your intended tonight with the fine manners I've gone to great lengths to instill in you."

Melissa put up a hand to still Sarah and looked at her mother in the mirror. "My intended?" Her hands fisted in her lap, the hairpins biting into her palm. "Just what does that mean?" A sick feeling of dread slithered through her middle.

"That means, young lady, that you have a responsibility as your father's only heir. We, your father and I, have been looking for a man capable of managing the fortune that will be yours. We have found such a man, and he will be in attendance tonight. He's of a good family and has an excellent head for business. It's a sound match. He'll manage your inheritance well."

"I should think an astute lawyer and a competent accountant could manage my funds quite well, and I wouldn't have to marry either of them." Heat tinged her cheeks. They'd found a husband for her? Based upon his financial prowess? "And what about my wants?"

"Nineteen is too young to know what you want. Trust me in this."

"Who is he? Do I know him?"

"No, I don't believe you've met him before. He's not much for social occasions. Doesn't go out much. And he's older than you, so he wouldn't have been in your social set. Your father has known him for years."

Older? How much older? Her thoughts galloped through a list of her father's friends. No one she would ever consider marrying came to mind. In fact, her father's business associates tended to be even older than he was. Visions of a rickety lecher danced between her and the mirror.

Mother checked the timepiece hanging from her lapel. "I don't have time to talk about it now. You'll meet him soon enough. Let Sarah finish your hair." Mother rose and pulled a velvet box from her dressing gown pocket. "I want you to wear this. It's perfect with your dress. And don't dawdle. You play at eight sharp."

"But, Mother—"

"Not another word on the subject, Melissa. Everything's already decided. The match is more than suitable, and your father will rest easy knowing an experienced businessman will be handling your inheritance. You should be thanking me. He'll be in the front row with your father, so play well." She swept out of the room, her words floating back over her shoulder.

Melissa stared at the door. A suitable match? To manage

the business? And she was only so much baggage that went along with the handshake? She bit her fingernail again. How humiliating. Who was this man? No doubt some middle-aged, paunchy boardroom bore with fat fingers and a cashbox for a heart.

"There, miss. You look lovely." Sarah tucked one last curl up and stepped back.

Melissa turned her head to one side then the other. Three navy ostrich feathers curled airily from the back of her upswept hair. A diamond pin held them firm and sparkled in the light of the gas globes overhead.

"I'll help you with your dress." Sarah took down the evening gown, slipping it from the padded, satin hanger.

Melissa stood, her mind awhirl. How could she get out of this? Could she pretend to be sick? The way her stomach was pitching at the moment, there would be no need to pretend. With numb fingers she loosened her pink dressing gown and laid it on the bed.

She jumped when the veranda door blew open. Chills raced up her bare arms. The cool October breeze off the lake wafted in, billowing the lace sheers. More than anything, she wanted to escape to the water. Perhaps the scrape and gurgle of the waves on the rocky shoreline would afford her the peace she needed to see a way out of this.

"Miss?" Sarah unfastened the bodice in the back and held out the gown.

How long had they been planning this? How could they choose a husband for her without even asking her what she thought? And a man she'd never met. What had they promised him? Well, it didn't matter. She wasn't going to go along with this. She stepped into the dress and slid her arms through the sleeves.

Sarah finished hooking her up the back and turned Melissa to look in the full-length mirror in the corner. "Ah, miss, the gentlemen won't be able to look away from you tonight."

Melissa smoothed her hand down the bodice, the fabric

slippery and cool under her palm. Yards of white satin gleamed in the lamplight. And over the bodice and skirt, a curly grillwork of appliquéd indigo velvet like a wrought iron silhouette. The train curled around her feet. How happy she'd been when she'd chosen this dress. She adjusted the neckline and settled the short white puffed sleeves.

"Here's your gloves, miss. Do you want a fan tonight?" Sarah held out the blue gloves, so dark they were almost black.

Melissa shook her head. "I can't wear the gloves while I play. Fold them up and take them downstairs and have one of the footmen put them on one end of the piano bench. And no fan. I feel so awkward when I have one."

While Sarah hurried on her errand, Melissa paced her bedroom, her mind a muddle. How did Mother expect her to play tonight after tossing a bomb like this at her? At the moment, Melissa couldn't even remember the music she'd selected. Surely Mother wasn't serious. And yet, Almina Brooke never said anything she didn't mean.

Sarah hurried back into the room, her apron crackling with starch.

Melissa sat on the low dressing stool once more and opened the blue velvet case. Nested on a bed of white satin, sapphires and diamonds twinkled mysteriously. Melissa's shoulders drooped. The jewels were perfect with the gown. Mother had thought of everything, as if Melissa were no more than an objet d'art to be shown off and admired. And sold to the highest bidder.

Sarah gasped at the jewels. "Oh, miss, they're wonderful! You'll be the most beautiful lady at the party. If those don't give you confidence, nothing would. Your parents will be so pleased, especially your father. He takes such great pride in you." She clasped the glittering stones around Melissa's throat.

They rested against Melissa's skin as cold and heavy as her heart. Melissa attached the dangling earrings, teardrop sapphires surrounded by diamonds.

Father did take great pride in her. Not an easy man to get close to, he did share her love of music and took pleasure in hearing her play.

"Sarah, please lay out the things I will need for later."

"Oh, surely not tonight, miss? Not with the concert."

"Yes, tonight. It will be tricky, but I'll manage. And, Sarah, thank you. I couldn't do this without your help."

Melissa regarded her reflection once more. No moping. Her chin lifted. She was more than a trinket to be trotted out by her parents and shown off. She'd play their game for a while tonight. And she would find a way out of this mess, or her name wasn't Melissa Diane Brooke.

three

Skimming the waves in *The Lady Genevieve*. Riding his thoroughbred at a gallop over fences. Sealing the deal on a new shipping contract. Jonathan ran through a list of things he'd rather be doing at the moment. He stood to one side of the brightly lit foyer watching his grandfather, impeccable in black tie, greet their hostess.

"Ah, Almina, you look radiant." The old rogue took her hand and kissed the air over her diamond-dusted knuckles. "May I present my grandson, Jonathan Kennebrae?"

Jonathan took the matron's offered hand and bowed. "How do you do, Mrs. Brooke?" He refrained from saying it was a pleasure to meet her, not wanting to lie. He took the measure of the woman his grandfather planned to make his mother-in-law. Handsome enough, he supposed, with high cheekbones and intelligent eyes. But calculation lurked in her glance as well. He swallowed and released her hand. Now he knew how a fish in a bucket felt.

"Lawrence is in the music room already. I've saved seats for you in the front row. I do hope you enjoy the concert. Do you like piano music, Mr. Kennebrae?"

Grandfather waved a hand. "Oh, call him Jonathan, and he enjoys piano music. We were just talking this afternoon about his past experiences at musical evenings such as this one, weren't we, Jonathan?" Grandfather sent him a wicked grin. "It seems he's particularly fond of nocturnes."

Jonathan stepped behind the wheelchair and clenched his fists around the steering bar. "Let's get you settled, Grandfather. I'm sure the music will begin soon." He directed the chair through the central hall, following the stream of guests. He leaned down and whispered, "Behave yourself. And

18

I'm telling you, if this girl plays "The Wedding March," I'm leaving so fast you won't see me for dust."

"Beautiful home, isn't it?" Grandfather ignored him, pointing to the staircase rising ahead and curving off to right and left galleries above. "Stunning architecture."

Jonathan barely glanced at the ornate stained glass, marble, and gilded woodwork. A trip to the firing squad had to be better than this. His collar tightened a notch. He wouldn't admit—even to himself—he was a tiny bit curious to see Miss Brooke.

Perhaps there was still a way out of this. But how? He'd done nothing but mull it over all afternoon. As Jonathan saw it, only one possible plan of escape might work. He had to find something in the girl's nature or background that made her unsuitable as a bride. While the idea of digging into a young woman's life for something unsavory didn't appeal to him, marrying her in order to keep Kennebrae Shipping appealed even less. And perhaps he wouldn't have to dig too deep. Everyone had a secret or two in his or her cargo hold.

The music room, with its golden parquet floor, Renaissance paintings, and high windows draped in heavy brocade, trumpeted wealth in every detail. Chairs had been set out in neat rows—there must have been at least fifty of them—and yet the room didn't seem crowded. Dominating the far end, a grand piano stood alone under a blazing crystal chandelier.

Jonathan scrutinized each young woman in the room, wondering which one was Miss Brooke.

Several business acquaintances stopped to speak with Grandfather. Michaels and Zahn, coconspirators in this marriage scheme, both greeted Grandfather with smiles and knowing looks. Jonathan schooled his features and pretended not to listen to them.

Lawrence Brooke stood near the front row, beckoning them to join him.

Jonathan regarded Brooke with a cold eye. Prior to this evening they had met only as business acquaintances—and that rarely. Tall, barrel-chested, with the look of a tenacious bulldog, Lawrence Brooke was a formidable man. Kennebrae Shipping had long sought his business but to no avail. Brooke shipped—through a Kennebrae rival—thousands of tons of wheat every year from Duluth Harbor and owned the three largest grain elevators on the docks. Added to that were more than two thousand miles of railroad through Minnesota and the Dakotas, all leading to Duluth. Brooke just might be the wealthiest man in a town that boasted more millionaires per capita than any other city in America.

"Abraham, glad you could make it. Going to be a fine evening." Lawrence clasped Grandfather's hand. "Jonathan."

When it was Jonathan's turn to shake hands, Lawrence Brooke's eyes bored into him, challenging and assessing. Jonathan tightened his grip, not backing down. He had nothing to be ashamed of, and he didn't care how intimidating Brooke tried to be.

Brooke broke the stare first, stepping back. "Welcome to Castlebrooke. Have a seat here beside me. Melissa will be down soon."

Melissa. So that was her name. Pretty name.

Jonathan wheeled his grandfather to the space of honor provided in the center of the front row. A business acquaintance caught his eye. "Excuse me for a moment." He nodded to Brooke and eased into the aisle.

"Don't be gone long." Grandfather's eyes flashed a warning.

"I won't."

Guests filed into the rows. Jonathan shook hands with one of his favorite clients near the back of the room, trying to ignore the way Grandfather and Mr. Brooke had their heads together in the front row. Maybe he could find a seat in the back of the room.

Almina Brooke made her way to the front. "Good evening, friends. Lawrence and I are so glad you could join us." She smiled, her dark eyes gleaming. "Without further ado, may I present our daughter, Miss Melissa Brooke, who will play for us tonight."

Polite applause from the audience.

A side door opened, and she entered.

Beautiful was the first word that sprang to Jonathan's mind. The second was *tiny*. His chest tightened. *Steady, man, you've seen pretty girls before.*

She had feathers in her hair. And her waist looked impossibly small. Jewels sparkled around her slender neck. Her train swept the parquet.

She stopped beside the piano, rested her hand on the edge, and scanned the crowd. Her gaze lingered on her parents then shifted to Grandfather. How old was she? Eighteen, nineteen at the most? She stood stock-still, staring at the front row. She reminded Jonathan of a songbird he'd once held in his hands, the tiny heart beating, the panic in the bird's eyes.

Blue. Her eyes were blue and fringed with dark lashes. Stunning.

Was it his imagination, or did her skin lose all color, washing as pale as the alabaster statue in the alcove behind the piano? She wavered a moment, and he thought she might faint. Then she swallowed and lifted her chin. Her breath came in short gasps, the jewels at her throat catching the light and winking it back at him as they shifted on her collarbones. She cast one desperate glance toward the door, her eyes locking on his for a long moment, then took her seat at the instrument. She looked like she might be ill.

Was he so disagreeable in looks that she nearly fainted? He admitted he was no dandy, but no one had actually gotten sick catching sight of him before. He scowled and shifted, lowering his arms to his sides.

For long moments she sat still, her hands in her lap. Not a breath of air stirred the ostrich feathers.

The audience began to fidget.

Mrs. Brooke turned her head and frowned, motioning for Jonathan to come take his seat. Maybe that's what the girl was waiting for.

His collar tightened another notch, and his mouth went

dry, feeling the audience's eyes on him as he slid into the chair next to his grandfather.

At last the girl lifted her fingers to the keys.

Beautiful and gifted. It took Jonathan less than a minute to reach that conclusion. She played with total concentration, evoking emotion through the music, breathing life into the piano with her own passion.

He didn't realize he'd been holding his breath until Grandfather elbowed him in the ribs and leaned close to whisper in his ear. "Might not be quite as bad as a hanging, huh?"

One glance at the man seated beside her father confirmed her worst fears. How could they? Her own parents. Why, it was monstrous. No one would blame her for refusing to obey in this instance. The man they had chosen as her husband was old! Old, gray, and in an invalid chair. It took every ounce of courage she possessed not to hike up the skirt of her couture gown and run from the room. Why, he was old enough to be her grandfather. Tears stung her eyes, and a hot coal burned the pit of her stomach.

Someone cleared his throat, startling her back to her surroundings. The concert. She must play. She raised her hands to the keys, noticed her fingers shaking, and forced them to be still.

Don't look over there again. You'll lose your nerve if you do.

Melissa pushed aside the panic and focused on the music. The melody took over, soothing, carrying her away from her troubles to a place that was beautiful and peaceful. Chopin always had that effect on her.

Each time she emerged from the music at the end of a piece, the audience applauded politely. Their approval sounded far away to Melissa, whose thoughts raced, fragments of worry scattering across her mind. Visions of false teeth and rheumatism medicines, watery eyes, and gnarled hands crowded in on her.

No, don't think about it. Think about the music. Lord, help me!

After the second encore, her mother rose and stood

beside the piano. "Thank you, thank you." She accepted the applause as if she had performed every piece herself. "No, no more tonight. Please join us next door in the ballroom for refreshments."

Melissa picked up her gloves and put them on, smoothing the satin up over her elbows. There was no escape now. How was she going to get through the rest of the evening, and when would she be introduced to her "groom?"

Guests crowded around her, complimenting her, thanking her for her performance. She deliberately kept her attention directed away from her parents and their guest of honor.

Finally her mother's hand snaked through the crowd and grasped Melissa's elbow. "I'm sorry to take her away from you, but there is someone waiting to meet her. Please, all of you, come enjoy the punch and delicacies next door."

The iron grip told Melissa her mother wasn't fooling. Melissa plastered a pleasant smile on her face and accompanied her mother to the front row of seats.

"Ah, Melissa dear, splendid performance tonight. I particularly enjoyed the last piece." Her father leaned down and kissed her cheek. "Abraham, I'd like to introduce you to my daughter, Miss Melissa Brooke. Melissa, this is Abraham Kennebrae of Kennebrae Shipping. I believe your mother mentioned he would be in attendance tonight?" Father's stare pierced her, demanding she behave herself and do him proud.

Melissa's mouth went dry. Mr. Kennebrae took her hand and gave it a squeeze, his brown eyes twinkling. "A pleasure, my dear. It did my old heart good to hear such beautiful music so excellently played. But it's even better to make the acquaintance of such a lovely young woman."

The old roué. Melissa withdrew her hand. Up close he was even older than she'd feared, his skin papery thin, his bones prominent. A shiver of nausea passed over her at the thought of being his wife. "Mr. Kennebrae." She nodded and sent her mother an imploring look. "I believe I'll check on the refreshments, if you will excuse me?"

Her father frowned. "Now don't run off just yet." He turned

to a young man who had his back to the group, speaking to another couple.

"Jonathan?" Father tapped the man on the shoulder. "Melissa, Jonathan came with Abraham this evening."

Melissa lifted her hand, her mind astir with extricating herself from Abraham Kennebrae.

The young man took her fingers in his.

Melissa's breath caught in her throat. She stared into a pair of velvety brown eyes fringed in heavy lashes. Dark hair touched his collar in the back. His cheeks and chin bore a hint of rough darkness indicating a heavy beard should he choose to grow one. A jolt sizzled up her arm as the heat of his hand penetrated her glove.

"Jonathan, may I introduce you to my daughter, Melissa? Melissa, Jonathan—"

A roar of laughter sounded from the ballroom.

"Oh, perhaps we should join them in the other room. We can continue our conversation over some refreshment."

The young man released her fingers, which still tingled strangely, and she lifted her hem to follow after her parents. He put his hands to the back of the chair to wheel Mr. Kennebrae to the reception. He must be her intended's caretaker. An invalid like Mr. Kennebrae would need someone to care for him.

"My dear, I do hope you'll sit beside me. We have so much to talk about." Mr. Kennebrae smiled up at her.

Though it chilled her to the bone to think of being his wife, she had to admit he had a certain charm. Like a favorite old uncle. She'd play the hostess for a while then find a way to escape. Tomorrow would be soon enough to confront her mother about this impossible situation. For tonight she'd be polite. "Of course, Mr. Kennebrae. I'd be delighted." She walked beside him into the brightly lit ballroom, but she couldn't resist glancing at the younger man.

Jonathan? Too bad he wasn't her parents' choice. She might have entertained the idea then.

four

"I would recommend you consider the Chicago property. Your docks in Detroit have paid off handsomely, not only in the fees you've saved on your own ships but in revenue received from other companies who use the docks. Chicago should pay as handsomely in the long run."

Jonathan took the batch of papers from his attorney and tried to focus on the columns. Where was his head today? Why couldn't he concentrate?

He blamed Grandfather. Grandfather and the conniving Brookes who'd cooked up this whole charade. The entire evening had been like a bad dream, unsettling and unreal.

Jonathan tried to loosen his jaw muscles and ignore his thoughts. Grandfather. The old codger sure enjoyed himself, shooting sly glances and addlepated grins at Jonathan every few minutes last night.

And the girl—she danced attendance on Grandfather as if he held the secrets of the ages. Why, she'd hardly paid any attention to Jonathan. Astute of her to study the old man. She must've been in on the plan from the start. Only Jonathan had been left in the dark.

And what a plan. Everything from the silver trays of canapés and savories to the masses of flowers surrounding the crystal punch fountain, every detail had been laid on to impress. One would have thought the king of England was visiting. And hadn't Grandfather lapped it up? Well, not Jonathan. He wasn't going to be shoved into this farce. Neither the sums involved nor the temptingly beautiful Melissa Brooke would entice him to stick his neck in this custom-designed noose.

"Mr. Kennebrae?"

Jonathan looked up to see eight pairs of eyes staring at

him. He looked from one board member to another, hoping for a clue as to what topic was under discussion. His lawyer inclined his head slightly toward the papers in Jonathan's hand. *Ah, thank you, Geoffrey.*

Jonathan pushed back from the table, his chair creaking. "Gentlemen," he said as he rose, "I apologize for my inattention. The decision on the Chicago property will require finesse. I agree that it would be a sound business investment. I wish I could go myself, but matters here require my presence." He turned to the director of finance. "Jacobson, you will travel to Chicago and talk to Summerton face-to-face. Tell him if we are to strike a deal, it must be done before the first of the year. I'll make decisions on the other two matters on the agenda and get back to you. That is all, gentlemen."

Jonathan turned his back and stared out the window at the street below and, beyond that, to the rock-strewn shore. "Geoffrey, I'd like you to stay."

Jonathan waited until the door closed before turning around. His lawyer and best friend lounged in his chair, rocking slightly, tapping his fingers on the padded arms.

"Geoff, I'm in an awful mess." Jonathan jammed his fingers through his hair.

"I wondered what had that normally razor-sharp brain of yours as dull as a lake stone. I felt like I was talking to a statue this morning." Geoffrey Fordham laced his fingers and rested his hands against his lean middle.

"Grandfather is the one who has dulled my wits. You wouldn't believe his latest scheme."

"It must be pretty bad to have you in such a lather. What's he doing? Getting married?"

Jonathan rubbed his palm across the back of his neck. "Hah, I wish. No, he's gone a step further. He's trying to maneuver *me* into matrimony."

Geoff blinked. "He's nagging you? Why should that bother you? He nags all the time."

"Not nagging, negotiating. He's negotiated my nuptials

without even bothering to tell me. He finally saw fit to enlighten me yesterday before dragging me off to meet the bride."

Geoff burst out laughing.

Jonathan scowled. "It's not funny. I tell you, I was poleaxed."

"I'm sorry. I can see you're worked up, but I have to wonder why. It isn't as if your grandfather's holding a shotgun to your head. He can't force you to marry anyone."

Jonathan shoved his hands into his pockets and leaned against the table. "He doesn't need a shotgun. He's got something a lot more powerful."

"What?"

"If I don't marry to his wishes, he'll disinherit me. Everything I've sweated blood for over the last eight years will be yanked out of my hands. I don't know how to do anything else, nor have I ever wanted to. But if I don't do as Grandfather says, there's no Kennebrae Shipping, no property in Chicago, no Kennebrae House, nothing. It will all go to Noah and Eli, as long as they, too, marry according to the master plan. He's already rewritten his will."

Geoff's eyes stretched wide, and his hands fell slack in his lap. "That's ridiculous. Is he mad? I knew nothing of this. Who prepared the will? Did he show it to you?"

"He's not mad. He's determined. Fixated on the subject. He intends to create a conglomerate of the wealthiest families in Duluth through marriage. And no, I didn't see the will. Wasserman probably drew it up. This place is rife with lawyers. Grandfather thinks you're not seasoned enough to handle his personal affairs, you know." Jonathan shook his head. "He says the will stands unless there is some legal or moral reason why the lady should prove unacceptable. But he must've had her checked out pretty thoroughly, or he'd never have thrown down the gauntlet like that. And he's not bluffing. Last night we made a social call on the woman he intends me to marry."

"So who's the blushing bride?"

"Miss Melissa Brooke, only daughter and heir of Lawrence

and Almina Brooke of Castlebrooke."

Geoff whistled low. "Brooke Grain and the Northstar Railroad? Ambitious of the old man. And you met her last night? Is she as beautiful as people say?"

"I'll let you decide. Grandfather and I are attending a party at Castlebrooke today. You can come along as my guest and meet her yourself. Then you can rack your brain for a way out of this mess."

❧

"Melissa!" Mother's sharp voice pierced a lovely dream. "It's well past time for you to be up. You need to get dressed."

Melissa rolled over and buried her head under the pillow. "Not yet, Mother." Quick hands yanked the pillow away, letting the brutal sunlight assault her eyes.

"Young lady, I do not understand your laziness. You'd sleep until noon every day if I let you. Now get up. Sarah's drawn a bath for you. I've invited a few friends for luncheon today. Including Mr. Kennebrae. It's been so unseasonably warm that I thought a terrace party would be nice."

Melissa groaned, yawning and stretching. Delightful. Another meeting with her fossilized groom. The lace cuffs of her nightgown flopped back as she lifted her arms over her head. "What time is it?"

"Past ten thirty. Now get moving. And wear the blue dress, the one with the matching parasol." Mother's shoes tapped on the glossy floor, and she swept out, closing the door with her customary bang.

At noon Melissa let herself out the back doors onto the terrace. The breeze ruffled the lace at her throat. She blinked in the bright sunshine glinting off the waves. Maybe she should go back in for her hat.

Too late. Mother advanced on her, grabbing her elbow and steering her toward the buffet table. "Melissa, come stand beside Mr. Kennebrae, and greet your guests."

What had Mother in such a flap? She was as jumpy as a frog with the hiccups, as their gardener would say. Her grip on Melissa tightened, and they all but ran to Mr. Kennebrae's chair. "No, no, not that side. Stand here."

Melissa found herself directed to stand between the wheelchair and. . .Jonathan. A curious tickle started under Melissa's heart and caused it to beat double-time. His eyes were as dark, his jaw as firm as she remembered. What was it about him that so appealed to her? She turned to greet Mr. Kennebrae. She swallowed hard. "Good afternoon, sir."

"My dear, so delightful to see you again. You're as pretty as a rose. As you should be on a day like today." He took her fingers between his gnarled palms and patted her hand, his dark eyes sparkling with life.

She forced a smile. This was getting beyond funny. If only she hadn't slept in, she could've confronted Mother about the absurdity of this situation. But the concert had lasted so long, and then she'd had to go—

Melissa intercepted a look from Mother who inclined her head toward Jonathan.

Melissa turned. "Good afternoon."

"Miss Brooke." His brows came down, his lips stiff. He looked like a thundercloud just before a squall. Perhaps his employer was giving him a bad time today. His animosity was clearly directed toward the man in the chair.

Again a pang of regret hit her middle. Such a waste, a handsome man like that, forced to be a body servant to an ambitious old man. Perhaps she would get a chance to talk to him later, make him feel more a part of the doings. But for now she must concentrate on being pleasant to Abraham Kennebrae so as not to embarrass her mother.

Knots of guests milled around the fountain and the gazebo and and across the green lawns. How many people had Mother invited? The staff spread luncheon on a buffet table laden with flowers, silver, and Mother's best linens. She certainly was laying it on thick for a mere garden party. And why were there no young people? Melissa recognized many of the women as friends of her mother's.

She put her finger to her mouth to bite her nails before she remembered she was wearing gloves. What was the matter with her? Just get through the luncheon then confront Mother head-on about this proposed engagement. It wasn't too late to back out. No one knew of the arrangements. A little patience and it would all be over.

❧

"She's beautiful. Are you sure you wouldn't rather just go through with it?" Geoffrey held out his plate to the servant and accepted the walnut chicken salad he offered.

Jonathan shook his head. "No. I won't be pushed into this. And besides, she's hardly even glanced my way. All her time's been spent cozying up to my grandfather. Guess she knows which way the tide's running." He vowed for the tenth time since arriving to stop letting his eyes wander to the girl seated beside his grandfather at the head table. She sat, stiff, her back straight. The breeze teased tendrils of hair on her neck, drawing his gaze again to her rosy cheeks, her lively eyes, her slender throat. *Stop it.*

Geoffrey cast a glance back over his shoulder, studying Jonathan's face. "Are you jealous?" He raised an eyebrow. "I'd swear your eyes have gone from brown to bright green."

"Don't be a fool. Jealousy would imply I wanted the girl for myself. Which I don't." Jonathan stopped abruptly when he intercepted a quizzical frown on the young woman serving the lemonade. "Let's go sit down."

They wove through the guests to the head table. Grandfather sent Jonathan a sharp look when he would've taken the chair farthest from Miss Brooke. Stifling his irritation, Jonathan set his plate down beside her.

She smiled at him, and he chided his heart for beating faster. *You're an idiot to let her affect you like this. Get ahold of yourself.*

The food was surprisingly good. He had not expected to be hungry. Of course he hadn't been able to eat his breakfast, downing several cups of strong coffee instead. This whole situation had him unsettled and well out of his routine. The sooner it was sorted out, the better.

Almina Brooke beamed on her guests, looking much like a lake bird who'd landed a large fish.

Jonathan intended to be the fish that got away.

"Abraham, I'd love to show you the late-fall roses." Almina dabbed her lips and waved to masses of blooms in an arrangement near the fountain. "I love having the conservatory. It means fresh flowers all year round." She gave a pointed glance in Jonathan and Melissa's direction.

Jonathan almost groaned. Not subtle, pushing them to be together like this.

"And, Mr. Fordham, would you be so kind as to join us?"

Geoffrey dropped his fork, midbite, with a clatter onto his plate. He snatched his napkin and wiped his mouth. "My pleasure."

Jonathan frowned at his lawyer for deserting him so eagerly. Geoffrey shrugged, wide-eyed and innocent. "I'll be back."

Almina adjusted her skirts. "Oh no, Melissa, there's no need for you to come along. Stay here and keep Jonathan company."

Jonathan sat staring at their retreating backs. Geoffrey gave him one sheepish glance over his shoulder then scuttled away behind the wheelchair. *Traitor.*

Melissa cleared her throat gently and laid her cake fork aside. She appeared about to speak but subsided. What was there to say, after all?

Well, he couldn't just sit here like a ninny. But frankly he had little experience talking to girls and none whatsoever in talking to prospective brides. "Kennebrae Shipping is doing well this quarter." *Oh, you idiot. Can't you think of anything better?*

"Is it? How nice." She gave him a puzzled glance then looked away in the direction Grandfather had gone.

"Four new Kennebrae ships will take to the lake this year. Business is booming." His mouth was like a leaky hatch cover. Words kept spewing out.

A small line formed between her dark arched brows, but she

nodded politely. "I suppose you know a lot about what goes on at the shipping offices, being so close to Mr. Kennebrae?"

"Yes, I attend all the board meetings and help oversee the day-to-day running of the company." Surely the girl knew that. She didn't think he was some sort of dilettante, sponging off the family business and doing no work at all?

Miss Brooke laid aside her napkin and took her gloves from her lap, inserting her hands and tugging them on with quick jerks. "You don't have to try to sell Kennebrae Shipping to me, sir."

Such a dolt. Of course she didn't want to hear about the company.

"I apologize, Miss Brooke. It's just that I'm more than a little concerned about this marriage business. My entire future's at stake here. I'd like nothing more than to call a halt to the entire affair, but I feel powerless. And no one is more stubborn than Abraham Kennebrae."

"Unless it would be my mother." She clapped her hand to her mouth and looked about her guiltily. "I'm sorry. I shouldn't have said it."

"Why not? It's true. The entire idea is ridiculous, and the sooner it's squelched, the better. I had no idea anything like this was in the works."

"I couldn't agree more. I've been so distressed since Mother informed me. I don't think I slept a wink until nearly dawn." She lifted her glass for a sip of lemonade.

Relief flooded through him. If neither of them wanted the marriage, then surely there was some way to call it off without jeopardizing his inheritance. "I'm so glad you feel that way. And it isn't just myself I'm thinking about here. The time to act is now, before the engagement is announced. After that it will be too late. Your reputation would suffer if the engagement was called off after the formal announcement. I wouldn't want that to happen to you. Not with you being a pawn in this entire chess match." He smiled at her, his blood heating when she returned the smile. Geoffrey was right; she was a beautiful girl, and in other circumstances, perhaps. . .

"Do you think there is a way to dissuade them? I don't see Mother budging. She's so pleased with herself. And my father, he's the king of his empire, but he's putty in Mother's hands. She's got his heart set on the match and in such a way that he thinks the entire thing was his idea."

"Don't blame it all on your mother. The old man had a hand in it, too." Jonathan jerked his chin in his grandfather's direction. Geoffrey pushed the chair along the flagstone path.

"I'm so glad I'm not the only one who sees the absurdity of the situation. I don't know what my parents were thinking. It's clear the age difference is too great. Why, it's scandalous."

That stung. How old did she think he was anyway? They couldn't be more than a dozen years apart. He didn't know much about such things, but he'd guess that was an average age spread for a married couple these days.

His attention was drawn from her by someone tapping a spoon against a glass.

"Goodness." She put her hand on his arm. He wondered if she even realized it. "Father's home in the middle of the day."

Lawrence Brooke tapped a glass again, and all conversation died down. He raised the glass. "Ladies and gentlemen, thank you for joining us on such a momentous day for our family."

Melissa's grip tightened on Jonathan's arm. He looked down at her, her face pale to the lips, her eyes wide. "Oh no," she moaned.

"My wife and I"—Almina had joined Lawrence Brooke, tucking her arm into his elbow and beaming on the crowd, her gaze lingering longest on Jonathan and Melissa—"are pleased to announce the engagement of our daughter, Melissa, to Mr. Jonathan Kennebrae. Please join us in congratulating the happy couple." He lifted the glass in their direction.

A polite wave of applause welled up.

Melissa stood, knocking her chair over onto the grass. She put her hand to her mouth, turning her head wildly from Jonathan to her parents then back again.

Jonathan rose slowly, easing up on numb legs.

"Kennebrae?" She whispered so low he had to stoop to hear her. "Your name is Kennebrae?"

"Of course it is. What else would it be?"

She blinked, staring at him. "But I thought—" Her throat spasmed as she tried to swallow. "I thought. . ."

He caught her just before she hit the grass in a dead faint.

five

Melissa slumped against him. Jonathan's arms reached around her, grabbing her to keep her from disappearing under the table. "Miss Brooke?"

When she didn't respond, he stooped, tucked his hand behind her knees, and lifted her in his arms. Her head fit into the crook of his shoulder, her breath dusting his neck. Jonathan looked around for a place to set her, but only the hard, white metal chairs met his eye.

Guests gaped, frozen in surprise. It had happened so fast that it seemed no one knew just what to do.

Except Almina Brooke. She advanced on him like a coming storm, eyebrows drawn down, mouth pinched in exasperation. "That foolish girl. Please accept my apologies, Mr. Kennebrae. Melissa, Melissa, stop playacting this minute."

Melissa didn't stir in his arms. He had a strange desire to clasp her tighter, turn his back, and shield her from her battleaxe of a mother.

People stared, leaning in, listening to every word.

"Mrs. Brooke, perhaps it would be best if we continued this discussion inside?"

Almina took a moment to realize her audience, plastered a concerned look on her face, and beckoned him. "Of course. Please bring her into the house."

Jonathan strode through the crowd, his anger, both at Almina Brooke and Grandfather, steaming through his veins. Of all the ridiculous positions.

A maid opened the terrace doors, her face crumpled in worry.

Jonathan nodded his thanks.

"Bring her through here, sir." The girl scurried ahead to a

pair of double doors on the left.

His footsteps echoed on the hard floors as he followed her into a gold and blue parlor.

The maid plumped a cylindrical pillow, beribboned and tasseled.

Jonathan felt a strange reluctance to let go of the burden in his arms. The delicate scent of roses drifted up from her hair. Dark lashes rested on her pale cheeks. Her lips parted, and he found himself staring at them. So soft, so perfect.

Someone cleared his throat.

Jonathan shook himself, dragging his gaze away from Melissa.

"Don't you think you should put her down?" Geoffrey lifted an inquiring brow toward Jonathan. He'd wheeled Grandfather into the house, and Abraham sat, covering his mouth with the side of his finger, a twinkle in his eye.

Anger surged through Jonathan. He laid Melissa on the davenport, easing his arms from beneath her. How dare his grandfather laugh at this situation of his own making.

Almina pointed to the maid. "Anne, don't just stand there, get a blanket or some smelling salts. Abraham, I'm so sorry. Melissa, so help me, if you're faking this, you're going to be— Jonathan, I can't believe—" The woman seemed to be mixing up her carping and apologizing.

He stepped between Almina and the sofa. "I assure you, madam, the girl has fainted. Perhaps you should send for a doctor instead of sputtering at her when she clearly can't hear you."

Almina's mouth opened and closed a few times, her eyes wide at his upbraiding. "Of course." She lifted her chin and bustled out of the room.

Jonathan knelt beside Melissa and took her hand between his. "Miss Brooke." Her face, lily-white, alarmed him. He chafed her hand, so small and cold. "Miss Brooke, are you all right?"

Her lashes fluttered, and her hand stirred in his.

Relief flooded him. He found himself looking into a pair of hazy sapphire eyes.

She blinked as if trying to understand where she was and why. Her mouth fell open, and she sat bolt upright, almost knocking him in the nose. "I'm supposed to marry you?" Her voice must've carried clear to the third floor.

Jonathan rocked back on his heels. "I assure you, Miss Brooke—"

"But I thought—" She turned to look at Grandfather. "Nobody told me. How was I supposed to know? You never said. Nobody ever said. Mother said Mr. Kennebrae. And I thought—" She broke off. "How did I get here?"

"You fainted, Miss Brooke." Geoffrey stepped closer, around the back of the brocade davenport. "Right after your father announced your betrothal. Jonathan caught you and carried you inside. Your mother's gone for some aid."

Melissa darted a look from one man to the other, finally resting her startled eyes on Jonathan. She looked at him as if he were a complete stranger.

"What is it that shocked you so, miss?" Geoffrey leaned over her. "Didn't your parents tell you of the engagement plans?"

"Of course." She stared into Jonathan's eyes, confusion, relief, and. . . Was that hope in her expression? "But Mother only said Mr. Kennebrae, and no one introduced Jonathan by his last name. I thought he was a companion or caretaker for the man I was to marry. I thought I was to become Mrs. Abraham Kennebrae."

Jonathan could hardly think above the laughter barking from both Geoff and Grandfather. He'd like to knock their heads together. No wonder she'd talked of age differences and the impossibilities of the union. Though where she got such an outlandish notion—

She broke their gaze, her face suffusing with color and her chin dipping. A single tear tracked down her cheek.

Pity stabbed Jonathan. "Enough, you cackling baboons. Get

out." He glared over his shoulder at Grandfather then shot Geoff a frown.

"Okay, okay." Geoff held up his hands in surrender. "We're going." He snickered and snorted, wheeling Grandfather from the room.

"Well," she whispered, gripping her hands in her lap, "it was an honest mistake. I'm so glad, though, that it's you instead of your grandfather. I mean, a fifty-year age difference. . ." She shuddered. "It would be enough to knock anyone into a faint."

Jonathan closed his eyes and rubbed his forehead with his fingertips. What a farce. At least she thought him a better catch than a seventy-year-old.

◆

How could she be so stupid? Melissa lay back against the cool linen pillows and stared at the plaster medallion on her bedroom ceiling. She flushed from her toes to the roots of her hair.

Well, who could blame her for misunderstanding? It wasn't as if anyone had given her the courtesy of a clear introduction. Anyone would've made the same mistake.

One bright spot shone out in all this mess. At least she wouldn't have to be Mrs. Abraham Kennebrae, a septuagenarian's wife.

The look on Jonathan's face though. Melissa groaned and slid down under the covers. What was the matter with her, babbling on like an idiot? She had no more brains than a trout.

A tap at the door.

Melissa peeked out. *Please don't be Mother again.*

She blew out a relieved breath as a tea tray emerged through the door. "Ah, Sarah, it's you."

"Yes, miss. How're you feeling?"

Melissa shrugged, sat up, and punched her pillows.

Sarah twitched the coverlet and set the tray down across Melissa's knees. "It was real romantic, him carrying you in like that. Don't you think so?"

Melissa flipped back her drooping cuffs and poured the hot, fragrant liquid. She sniffed the delicate aroma. Romantic? How romantic was it to drop into a dead faint in the arms of a man she had no idea she was engaged to?

"I'm sorry I couldn't be here when the doctor came. Mrs. Brooke set me to clearing up outside. There was lots to clean up after the guests finally left."

Melissa set the cup down, rattling it against the saucer. More sickening embarrassment swirled through her. She put her palms over her eyes and dragged her hands down her face.

"Don't fret, miss. I'm sure things will work out."

Melissa crumbled her scone on her plate. How could she look either of the Kennebraes in the eye ever again?

"It's almost ten o'clock. Do you want me to send word to Britten's that you won't be coming tonight?"

Melissa threw her arm up over her eyes. No one had ever told her that acute shame drained the strength from you like grain from a leaky railcar. She wanted nothing more than to pull the covers over her head and sleep, for at least a decade or two, until the whole thing blew over. "No, Sarah. It's not like I'm really sick. I'll go."

She threw back the covers and slid her feet to the floor. At least the darkness would hide her blush.

❧

Jonathan paced Grandfather's office. "This is all your fault, pulling strings like Machiavelli. Piled so much stress on the girl she fainted."

"Now, son, you can't blame me for this. Her mother should've been clearer. I had no idea that little girl would think. . . Well, I'm flattered—I really am—but it never entered my head she'd react like that. Frankly, if I was forty years younger, I'd give you a run for your money." The old rogue's eyes twinkled, his cheeks flushed with pleasure.

Jonathan stopped pacing. "Be serious, won't you? What possessed you to allow the Brookes to announce the engagement in front of all those people? I should've denied involvement in your schemes right there."

He resumed prowling the carpet, hands jammed in his pockets, anger boiling in his middle. When he thought of her pale face on his arm, bloodless lips parted, her hair falling out of its pins. . . The protective rush of feeling that sprang up inside him had startled him. That the feelings hadn't faded surprised him more.

"You wouldn't do that, Jonathan. Kennebrae Shipping means too much to you. I knew it would. I don't know why you're resisting this so much. She's a nice girl, beautiful and good. She'll make you a fine wife. You have nothing to complain about."

"Nothing to complain about? You don't get it, do you? I want to be free to choose my own bride. I want to marry someone I love and who loves me in return."

"Love? Love isn't necessary to a marriage. Common interests, background, and social standing make for a sound union. I didn't love your grandmother when I married her. That came later."

"I surely don't want to marry someone on the off chance that someday she will love me. But that's going to be more difficult now, isn't it? Everyone at the party heard the announcement. How am I going to get out of this now?"

"Not just everyone at the party." Grandfather chuckled, rubbing the cover of his pocket watch with his crepe fingers. "It will be in the *Duluth Daily News* and the *St. Paul Pioneer Press* tomorrow morning. I imagine engagement gifts will begin arriving at Castlebrooke shortly after that."

Jonathan gritted his teeth so hard that he feared they might crack. His jaw ached from the strain of not yelling. He was caught in a whirlpool, spiraling down to the moment when he'd say, "I do."

He turned to his grandfather, striving to modulate his voice. "Don't think this is the end of it." He stalked from the room, Grandfather's delighted cackle following him down the hall.

If only he could speak to Miss Brooke. . .Melissa. He

supposed since they were now formally engaged, though without benefit of a proposal, he could call her "Melissa." Embarrassment heated his face. She'd thought him a servant, his grandfather's lackey. Though, truth be told, what else was he, getting backed into a situation like this?

Knowing she didn't want the engagement either pricked his pride. But why? He should be relieved. He shook his head and mounted the stairs to his rooms on the third floor. Foolish to be piqued by the rejection of a woman he didn't even want to marry.

He opened the door to his suite, familiarity and comfort wrapping around him. The rest of the house might be Grandfather's, but this was his domain. Gas lamps lit the walnut paneling. Dark blue and burgundy rugs covered the polished floors. Watercolors of ships and the lake in gilded frames brightened the walls.

Jonathan dropped his keys and coins into a wooden bowl on the pie-crust table beside his favorite chair. The chair creaked a familiar welcome as he stretched his legs. The papers from this morning's board meeting lay in tidy piles on his desk in the corner, chiding him about his lack of attention to them. He had never gone to bed without finalizing meeting reports, but tonight he couldn't concentrate on anything.

A knock at the door. "Sir?"

"Yes, McKay?"

"Telegram, sir."

Jonathan took the envelope and tapped his thigh with it. When the door closed behind the butler, he slit the envelope and unfolded the stiff paper.

Great, Noah would be held up in Detroit. Just when Jonathan needed one of his brothers to talk to. Noah was clever and a problem solver, using light banter to hide his keen mind. If anyone could find a way out of this mire, Noah could. And in such a way that would preserve Melissa's reputation and allow Jonathan to keep control of Kennebrae Shipping.

He wadded the telegram and fired it at the hearth. No

matter where he turned, he was alone, his back to the wall. Give up Kennebrae Shipping, or give in and marry Melissa Brooke.

What if she was the one who called off the wedding? He couldn't be blamed for that, could he?

Sitting here was getting him nowhere. He needed to talk to her.

A strip of light showed under Grandfather's second-floor bedroom door. Probably in there hatching up some new misery regarding Jonathan's firstborn.

McKay met him near the front door. The man had an uncanny sense of where everyone in the house was at all times.

"Shall I call the carriage, sir?"

"No. I'll walk. Don't wait up." Jonathan snatched his hat and topcoat from the hall tree. A quick look through the canes and umbrellas sorted out his favorite, silver-topped walking stick.

A brisk wind off the lake fluttered lapels and caused his pant legs to snap. He anchored his hat and set off up Superior Street.

An automobile puttered by, the streetlights gleaming off its shiny metal. Behind it, slower, a delivery wagon rattled up the road, horses' hooves clopping on the damp pavement.

He tossed a look over his shoulder, picking out the silhouette of the new canal bridge. The *Kennebrae Jericho* lay at anchor just outside the harbor awaiting morning to enter the port. A light burned from her pilothouse, casting a glow in the hazy night air.

Jonathan knew the location, cargo, and manifest of every one of the twenty-eight Kennebrae ships on the lake. He knew their histories, their captains, their capacities. When one went down in a storm, he mourned not only the loss of life and income but the ship itself. Each was an individual, unique, a member of the Kennebrae Shipping family. He chose their captains with all the care of a protective parent.

His standards were high, and a job with Kennebrae gave a man status in the community and on the lake.

He couldn't walk away. It would be like cutting out his heart.

I need an escape, Lord. I can't seem to find my way through. Legally Grandfather's got me tied to the mast. I've worked so hard to build the company up. You know how scared I was, how green, fresh out of college, with Grandfather lying in bed unable to speak a word. But I saw it in his eyes. Pleading with me to hold on to all he had worked for. And with Your help, I did it. You've blessed the business in so many ways. I can't find words to thank You.

Jonathan cut across a side street with swift strides, continuing up the tree-lined sidewalk. His prayers came as fast as his steps.

Surely You wouldn't have brought me this far, allowed me to be this successful, then take it all away? Help me find a way out of this. Change Grandfather's mind, or show me some way of escape.

Castlebrooke loomed ahead, its front porch illuminated by two carriage lamp sconces under the porte cochere. Strangely no lights shone from the windows on the front of the house.

Jonathan slipped his hand inside his overcoat and palmed his pocket watch. He flipped open the engraved gold lid and turned the timepiece toward the fuzzy glow of the gaslight on the corner. Well after ten o'clock. What a buffoon. Of course there were no lights in the house. Why hadn't he thought of the time before he left Kennebrae House?

He glanced around him and backed out of the light into the shadows of a high iron fence. If anyone saw him lingering out here, he'd look like some love-struck fool sighing his soul up to the boudoir of his beloved. Not a chance. He gripped his walking stick until his fingers ached, trying to ignore the flush of embarrassment creeping up his chest.

He tugged his hat down and drew his overcoat collar up to hide his face. He took one look over his shoulder to ensure no one had seen him then stepped onto the curb. He'd cross the street and circle the block heading west.

A click, a creak, and the soft glow of candlelight stopped him in his tracks.

"Be careful. The fog will be coming in afore you get back." A woman's voice.

"I will. Don't worry, Sarah. You don't have to wait up for me. I'll be very late."

Jonathan slid into the shadows once again and peered through the hedge inside the fence. The front door of Castlebrooke closed, the light disappearing with a sharp *snick*.

Tap, tap, tap. Shoes on the curved brick driveway. Whoever was coming would pass by him on his left. He eased farther into the leaves spreading over the sidewalk until his back pressed against the iron bars of the fence. Then he stopped. What would be more embarrassing? To be found on the sidewalk outside Melissa's home or to be discovered skulking in the bushes? Enough of this foolishness. If anyone saw him, he'd just explain. He was out for an evening stroll. That was all.

A trim figure hurried through the gate and turned away from him, not even glancing in his direction. She carried a valise and swept under the street lamp. At the corner she paused and looked up.

Melissa Brooke.

Now where would she be going at this hour? And alone?

Curiosity won out over possible embarrassment, and he followed her at a discreet distance.

She kept her head down, not looking around at all. Did she have no care for her own safety?

He hastened his steps to close the distance a bit more.

A block from her home, she drew up to the same delivery wagon Jonathan had seen earlier. Britten's Bakery. A bakery delivering at this hour? More puzzlement. Without the slightest hesitation she handed her valise up to the unseen driver and climbed aboard.

The wagon set off at a sedate pace that Jonathan found easy to match. A suitable explanation for her behavior eluded him, but his curiosity was aroused so he couldn't leave off trailing her. When they passed Kennebrae House, he gave it barely a glance before hurrying after the wagon.

They entered the deserted business district. The horse's hooves clopped in a damp, gritty cadence on the now slick streets, echoing off the stone and brick buildings on either side of the road. Jonathan had to meld into the shadows when the wagon pulled to a stop on the steep slope of Lake Avenue.

She stepped from the wagon with her bag and set off at a brisk pace down the sidewalk toward Minnesota Point.

Lights reflected in yellow ribbons on the black water. But for the sound of the wagon turning around and heading back up the street, Jonathan was sure he would be able to hear the sucking and slapping of the waves on the rocky shore.

What business would a respectable woman have at the harbor in the middle of the night? Was it something he could use to reason with Grandfather that she was an unsuitable bride?

On the corner of Lake Avenue and Buchanan Street, across the street from his own shipping offices, someone stepped out of the doorway of a three-story brick building. He couldn't tell at this distance if it was a man or a woman.

What was Melissa doing? She walked right up to the person, and the two embraced.

A pang nicked Jonathan's heart. He stopped. The light was too poor to make out the person's face. He refused to acknowledge the disappointment that his search for something questionable in her background had been so shockingly easy to find. Somehow she hadn't seemed the type to have a sordid secret. He chided himself for being taken in by a pair of wide blue eyes and an innocent expression.

Time to confront her. He took a fresh grip on his walking stick and lowered his collar.

Two steps and the world went black.

six

Melissa turned at the sound of something heavy hitting the pavement behind her. What on earth? Two figures bent over something on the sidewalk. She knew them. "Wait here out of sight," she cautioned her companion. "Peter, Wilson, what is it?" She called out to the two boys who weren't yet out of their teens.

"I told ya there was someone following us. He trailed you all the way from your house. We made like we was turning around, but Wilson dropped off the back of the wagon and followed him. I parked up there and hustled down to help if he needed it." Peter wiped his nose with the base of his thumb. His forelock fell over his eyes.

"Yeah." Wilson stuck out his chest a bit. "Ma told us not to let anyone bother you. This fella was hiding in the bushes in front of your house."

Alarm fluttered in her middle. She grabbed the young men's arms. "Did you kill him? What have you done?"

"Naw," Peter scoffed. "We just banged him on the head with this. Show her, Wilson."

Wilson opened his hand to reveal a blackjack, sinister and shiny. "He'll have a wicked headache when he wakes up, that's all."

"Who is he?" She leaned over but couldn't see the man's face.

"Dunno, but he has on some swank clothes." Wilson squatted and turned the man over so he lay on his back.

Melissa clapped her gloved hand to her mouth to stifle a cry. "Oh no!" She looked up at the brothers. "Not him!"

Jonathan Kennebrae lay sprawled on the pavement, his hat

knocked off, his coat twisted around him. A welt rose on his right temple.

"You know him?"

She nodded and blew out a breath. What were they going to do now?

"Who is he?"

Her mind whirled as she sought to come up with a suitable answer. Finally she decided on the straightforward truth. "He's my fiancé."

Peter snatched off his hat and whacked Wilson with it. "You nincompoop. I told you we shouldn't hit him on the head. You done knocked out the fella she's gonna marry."

"Well, how was I supposed to know, him following her like that? He looked like a pickpocket with his collar all turned up and his hat pulled down low."

Melissa looked up the street. Nothing moved; no lights shone in the buildings. She tugged on her fingers, twisting them inside her gloves.

"What do you want us to do with him? Should we wake him up?"

"No, don't do that. Let me think." How did Jonathan come to be following her anyway? What did he know?

She stood and smoothed her coat. "You must take him home. Peter, go get the wagon. Bring it here, and you and Wilson load him in and take him—" No, they couldn't take him all the way home. Not in the bakery wagon. Someone was sure to see it, and tongues would be wagging. She couldn't afford anyone wondering why Britten's Bakery made deliveries at midnight.

"Take him a couple blocks from his home—you know the place, Kennebrae House—and park where there are no streetlights. Carry him home from there. If anyone asks, just say your friend isn't feeling well. There's a veranda on the north side of the house. We saw it when we went by. There's bound to be some furniture there. Find a davenport or chair.

Don't just dump him on the floor." Guilt and urgency made her voice waver.

"Can we go through his pockets first?"

"No! You've done enough already!"

Peter frowned and turned to go.

She caught him by the sleeve. "I'm sorry. I shouldn't snap at you. I do appreciate you looking out for me. But hurry. We must get him home. If he wakes up, he'll be full of questions I don't want to answer."

"We'll get him home. And we'll come see you back safe, too. Don't leave without us. Ma'd skin us if we let you walk home in the dark." He whirled and ran up the street.

"Help me move him, Wilson. He looks so uncomfortable." She put her hands to Jonathan's broad shoulders. Why hadn't she noticed before what a muscular man he was? The smell of shaving soap drifted up as she put her cheek near his face and lifted, easing him over. "Give me your jacket."

Wilson shrugged out of his coat and handed it to her.

She folded it and gently lifted Jonathan's head to pillow it on the bunched cloth. He looked pale to her, and the welt stood out in an angry red line.

Please, God, don't let him be seriously hurt. For his own sake and theirs. They were just trying to protect me. And don't let him wake up before they get him home. He wouldn't understand why I'm here, and he certainly wouldn't understand why the boys knocked him out.

"Miss Brooke, I think you should go. I'll wait here with him till Pete gets back with the wagon." Wilson waved her away.

Torn, she smoothed back Jonathan's hair and placed her hand on his chest. His heart beat slow and steady, and his chest rose and fell rhythmically. Perhaps he would be all right.

Wisps of fog curled along the pavement. With the wind dying down, it would shroud the city in another half hour or so.

"Stay with him, Wilson."

"I will."

She stood once more and hurried up the street, looking back every few steps. Fog swirled about her feet, creeping up the street to envelop Wilson and her injured fiancé.

Had she done the right thing?

❧

Jonathan stifled a groan as his shoulder hit the floor of the wagon. He kept his eyes closed. Rough hands shoved his legs inside while boots clambered over him. The conveyance lurched forward.

Couldn't even put him on a seat. Who were these hooligans? The faint smell of yeast floated over him. Jonathan gritted his teeth and fought swirling nausea.

"Dunno why we can't at least toss his pockets. It's not like he can't afford it."

Jonathan fought to maintain consciousness.

"We can't because she said so, that's why. You have rocks for brains? If we rob him, the police'd be after us. They might be anyway, thanks to you."

Police? No, he couldn't do that. Too embarrassing.

"Hey, you were the one who said we had to stop him. What else was I supposed to do?"

"I figured we'd just scare him a bit, you know, maybe throw a couple punches. Never figured he was Miss Brooke's intended."

Jonathan wanted to sit up and protest being called Melissa Brooke's intended, but he couldn't muster the energy. His limbs felt like sails with no wind.

"Dunno why he should be following her anyhow. Not in the middle of the night. You think he knows?"

Knows? Knows what? Blackness engulfed him.

Something jostled Jonathan awake. Hands grabbed his legs and arms and hauled him into the night air.

Jonathan opened one eye a crack. He was sitting on the pavement. Several sets of wagon wheels appeared, merged, and separated in his vision as he tried to focus.

"Come on, get him up." His arms were jerked up and slung

over the shoulders of his captors. "And don't forget that fancy cane."

His feet dragged the pavement, his weight hanging from his shoulders. Why couldn't he walk properly?

"Let's put him down and get a better grip. He's too heavy to carry this way."

The men lowered Jonathan to the ground and shifted positions. One grabbed his feet; the other slid his hands under Jonathan's arms and laced them across Jonathan's chest.

"Next time, you get the shoulders. He weighs a ton."

Jonathan wanted to argue. He wasn't fat. His tongue wouldn't form the words.

"Stop your whining. We're almost there."

Almost where? Jonathan tried to ask, but the words came out in a jumble.

"Hurry up. He's coming around."

"She said the side veranda."

Shoes on pavers. A street lamp. Trees.

Thud. His body hit the floor hard.

"She said to put him on the bench."

"You wanna be here when he wakes up? Let's go. We gotta get back to Miss Brooke anyway, before she decides to walk home alone."

Their footfalls receded.

Jonathan opened one eye. The silver head of his walking stick lay inches from his nose. It was too much effort to move. He slid into the darkness again.

Just after daybreak Jonathan held an ice pack to his temple, wincing at the chilling sting.

McKay set a tray of coffee at his elbow and retreated to stir the fire in the grate.

Jonathan longed to go to bed, but the chorus of anvils in his head made sleep impossible. Sitting here thinking was difficult enough.

Steam wisped from the coffee cup. Two sugars, just as he liked it. Then he noticed the glass of water and two headache powders on the tray. McKay was a saint. Jonathan mixed the powers and downed the opaque liquid in three swallows. He eased his head back onto the antimacassar.

Weak light streamed through an opening in the drapes. Sunrise. What day was it? Sunday. He groaned. Soon he must make an effort to gather himself and get to church. He hadn't missed in years, and he wasn't going to now. The explanations would be too humiliating.

Cramped muscles protested every movement. The chilly night and hard flagstones had done him no favors. Well, one, he supposed. The swelling on his head was much reduced. A look in his shaving mirror had shown him a slightly discolored bump along his hairline but not the grotesquely bruised goose egg he'd feared.

Groggy impressions of rough hands, grunts, and clattering wheels on pavement flitted around his memory, tantalizing but encased in fog.

"Sir, is there anything else I can do for you? Shall I summon the police?" McKay refilled Jonathan's cup, his pale blue eyes disturbed, his brow furrowed. "Such a dreadful thing, to be robbed like that."

"It wasn't a robbery."

"Yes, sir." He bowed, too experienced with the Kennebraes to question further. Good man. Jonathan closed his eyes.

No, not a robbery. He still had his watch, his walking stick, and even his wallet inside his breast pocket. And no thief would've brought him home. Jonathan couldn't blame last night's doings on a crook.

No, he lay the blame squarely where it belonged. At the feet of the beautiful Melissa Brooke.

seven

McKay's powders barely put a dent in the pain. Jonathan pushed Grandfather up the center aisle of the sanctuary, grateful for the handle on the wheelchair to help prop himself up. Bright prisms of color from the stained glass windows danced in the air of the vaulted ceiling high overhead.

Jonathan wheeled the chair into the special nook Grandfather had commissioned when he knew he would be an invalid the rest of his life. Four rows from the front on the left side, where the Kennebraes had sat since the church was erected twenty years before. Jonathan stepped into the pew and sat down, biting back a groan. Perhaps if he kept his eyes closed, people would think he was praying.

Grandfather nudged Jonathan's elbow.

He opened his eyes.

"She's here. Stand up and be nice."

"Who's here?"

"Your bride, you imbecile. Almina and I thought it best that your bride's family attend church with us this morning."

With the organ music in the background and his jumbled thoughts in the foreground, Jonathan had a fleeing moment of panic. Then he laughed at himself. No, it wasn't the wedding yet.

Lawrence Brooke strode up the aisle, Almina on his arm, but Jonathan looked right past them. There she was. He sucked in a breath, hit afresh at her beauty.

She wore a gown the color of his beloved lake, trimmed in lace like whitecaps. Her hair swept up from her neck, and a wide-brimmed hat trimmed with a single, white silk rose covered her head. Very ladylike.

Jonathan nodded to the Brookes, husband and wife.

Almina frowned when Melissa seated herself firmly at

the far end of the pew and did not make eye contact with Jonathan.

It suited Jonathan just fine. Until he had his headache and his temper under control, she'd best stay out of his line of sight. He ignored the black looks Grandfather shot from under his bushy white eyebrows.

"Our text for this morning is found in Proverbs 21:1." The pastor opened his Bible and spread it on the podium.

Jonathan opened his own Bible to the passage, the familiar sound of thin papers rustling around him.

"The king's heart is in the hand of the Lord, as the rivers of water: he turneth it whithersoever he will."

Anytime now, Lord, if You could turn Grandfather's heart, I'd sure appreciate it. It's going to take an act of Yours because he's so stubborn. It would be easier to drink Lake Superior dry than change his mind once he's set on something.

Jonathan's thoughts multiplied even as his headache receded. What was she up to, down near the harbor bridge at night? She had met someone in the shadows, that much he remembered. Was it a man? But for what purpose. Romantic? Illegal? Certainly clandestine. He grimaced. Unsavory to say the least. But if true, it might be his escape.

Before he realized it, the sermon was over.

The congregation stood to sing the final hymn, and then the pastor gave the familiar benediction. "And before we depart this Lord's Day, I have an announcement for you all. Please give your best wishes to Jonathan Kennebrae and Melissa Brooke who celebrated their engagement this week. I've been informed that the wedding will take place at Castlebrooke on December 16. Congratulations, Jonathan and Melissa!"

Jonathan closed his eyes, his hands gripping the pew ahead of him. Organ music welled up and out, crashing around him.

Grandfather nudged him in the knee.

His eyes flew open. "You set the wedding date?" He spoke through stiff lips, his body clammy and tense. "What else have you done? Arranged a honeymoon? Named our firstborn?"

Grandfather's chuckle infuriated him. "No, son, but I wouldn't be hurt if you named him after me."

"It's too much. You've gone too far."

Grandfather sat back, looking up at him with dark, glittering eyes. "Take it like a man. Folks are coming to greet you. Think of Melissa. If you cause a scene here, it will ruin her."

Melissa. He'd completely forgotten her in his anger. Where was she? Had she escaped? He looked over the heads for a blue hat with a white rose.

Almina had Melissa by the elbow, urging her to stand beside Jonathan in what became a sort of informal receiving line.

Melissa looked so pale that Jonathan feared she might faint again. People crowded around, shaking their hands, clapping him on the shoulder, wishing them well. What a farce.

Almina stood, beaming, on the far side of Melissa, and Grandfather sat at Jonathan's side accepting congratulations, hemming them in and preventing either of them from bolting. Very clever.

But most disconcerting was Lawrence Brooke who stood behind them both. Jonathan's imagination conjured up a shotgun held neatly to his back.

The wedding was on.

❧

"What do you think of her?"

Melissa jerked her chin up. It took a moment to realize Father wasn't talking about her. He waved his arm wide over the deck of the *Almina Joy*, his newest yacht.

Jonathan stood at his side, face to the breeze, staring out over the lake. His legs braced apart with the roll of the waves.

Sunday luncheon with guests on the family yacht had always been an enjoyable ritual for Melissa. Until today. The movement of the boat on the water only enhanced the uneasy feeling under her heart. And every time she caught sight of the discoloration on Jonathan's temple, her guilt grew.

How much did he know? Why had he followed her? What

would he do now? Did he know who had hit him? She gripped her coat tight at the throat.

"Tell me more about him. He's so handsome." Zylphia Montrose clutched Melissa's arm as they strolled the deck. She leaned in conspiratorially. "Tell me everything."

"There's nothing to tell, really. I'd rather hear about your trip to New York."

Zylphia's eyes lit up. "Oh it was a wonderful time! We stayed at the Chelsea and dined at Delmonico's. We even saw Mark Twain there." She squeezed Melissa's arm harder. "He was in the bar, and Mother and I only got a peek, but I'm sure it was him. When I asked the waiter, he got all sly and secretive and said it was against policy for the staff to discuss the guests."

Melissa smiled and nodded, glancing over her shoulder at Father and Jonathan. What were they discussing? Surely he wouldn't ask Father about her late-night excursions, would he? Panic fluttered up.

"I'd better go to Jonathan, Zyl. I wouldn't want him to think I'd abandoned him. Besides, you'll be wanting to work on your next conquest. Mother's invited some very nice, eligible men today."

"None as eligible as the one you snagged." Zylphia gave her a grin. "If he was mine, I don't think I'd stray too far either."

Melissa buttoned her long coat with chilly fingers. This could likely be the last afternoon sail of the season. Indian summer had lasted through mid-October, but the nice weather wouldn't stay much longer. The *Almina Joy* would be dry-docked in the boathouse, wrapped tight to wait until ice-out in the spring.

Jonathan gave her barely a glance when she came to stand beside him. Her father, however, beamed broadly. She breathed a sigh of relief. Jonathan couldn't have mentioned last night. At least not yet.

Father tucked his fingers into his vest pockets. "You look a picture today, Melissa. You've always been a good sailor." He turned to Jonathan. "Loves the water. That's a good thing, eh? I hear sailing is one of your interests. You and Melissa will have to spend more time together. I'm sure you have lots of other things in common." He clapped Jonathan on the back.

Melissa caught the slight wince that passed over Jonathan's face at the impact. His head must still be hurting him.

"Yes, we have a lot to talk about." Jonathan held out his arm to Melissa. "Perhaps you'd fancy a stroll on deck?"

Perfect. She could get him away from Father. She tucked her hand into his elbow, surprised at the play of muscles under her fingertips and the warmth that radiated through his coat to her chilled fingers. "Let's walk to the bow. I like to be near the front whenever I can."

He led her up the starboard side, past the forward sail hatch, to the prow.

A deckhand nodded to them and finished winding a rope. He touched his cap and backed away. Father claimed to love being on the lake, but he did none of the sailing himself. A captain and crew of six manned the *Almina Joy*.

"As your father said, we have much to discuss, don't we, Melissa?"

It was the first time she could recall his using her given name. The way he said it didn't sound too friendly. More like a warning shot across her bow.

She released his arm and stepped to the rail, turning her back on him. "Father says you enjoy sailing. Do you have a vessel?"

"Yes, the *Lady Genevieve*, a seventy-four footer. She's tied up at the dock at the house. But I didn't bring you up here to talk about boats. Let's stop pretending, shall we?"

"Pretending?" Melissa looked at him over her shoulder. Her heart picked up the pace. She turned to face him.

"Yes, stop acting like you don't know about last night. You owe me an explanation, and I intend to get one." He loomed over her, arms crossed on his chest, the wind ruffling his dark hair.

"Mr. Kennebrae, I don't owe you anything." She backed up until the rail embraced her waist.

He stepped forward, trapping her neatly. "Yes, you do. For the moment, I'm your fiancé. That entitles me to some answers." His eyes trapped hers as easily as his body hemmed her in. He put a hand to the rail on either side of her and leaned forward.

She eased back and tried to see over his shoulder. Where had everyone gone? "This engagement is a farce, and you know it. You said yourself you were looking for a way out of it."

"And I may have just found it. You've handed it to me on a platter." He looked grim, not like she thought he should at such wonderful news.

"How have I done that?" His eyes mesmerized her, and the words came out breathlessly.

He lowered his head to whisper in her ear. His breath tickled her cheek, warming it to tingling. "One word from me and the engagement will be off. I only need to mention the fact that you are in the habit of traipsing down to the harbor at night to meet a man and"—he snapped his fingers—"no more wedding."

She blinked, her mouth dropping open. "Is that what you think? That I—"

"What else am I supposed to think? It was obvious from your bodyguards' conversation when they took me home last night that this wasn't the first time you took yourself down there. And who was that in the shadows? I may not be in favor of this engagement, but I will not be made a fool of for its duration."

Relief crashed over her like a wave against a pier. He was off base. So far from the truth as to be laughable. But she still sailed dangerous waters. "How much did you hear?"

"Enough to know you're in trouble right up to your pretty little neck."

His patronizing manner infuriated her. She narrowed her eyes and put her hands on her hips. "Mr. Kennebrae, I can assure you, my late-night jaunts have nothing to do with meeting a lover. That you jumped to that conclusion does you no favor in my eyes."

His hands moved from the rail to her arms. "It was not a far leap. Can you deny that I found you in the presence of more than one man in the middle of the night on Lake Avenue? What were you doing down there if not an assignation? Aside from your minders, who was the person you embraced in the shadows?"

"None of your business. Now unhand me, you ungallant oaf."

His grip tightened for a moment, his eyes angry and hot. Then his hands dropped to his sides, and he stepped back. "Very well, you give me no choice. I shall have to discuss this with your father. I'll get out of the engagement in such a way that my grandfather cannot object, and you'll find your night ramblings put to an end."

To his credit there was no triumph in his look. . .only sadness and disappointment. Had he really been hurt thinking she was seeing someone else?

But if Father found out, it would be disastrous. Time for a little diplomacy. "Please, don't tell Father. Won't you accept my word that I'm not seeing another man?" She smiled up at him, tilting her head and giving him an entreating look.

"I cannot. If for no other reason than your safety. Those two delinquents you use as bodyguards, while effective last night, aren't to be counted on in real trouble. Something far worse might happen to you wandering in that part of town at that hour. Then there is your family to consider. If someone finds out, your reputation will be in tatters—and not only yours but, as your fiancé, mine as well. I'll be a laughingstock. And I can't imagine what your mother would say. She's a social dragon as it is." He took her hands in his, all anger wiped away. "Come clean, Melissa. If it isn't another man, then what is it?"

"I can't tell you. You wouldn't understand."

"Try me. You must tell me if for no other reason than to clear your name."

She twisted her hands, staring at the shore slipping by, the waves lapping on the rocky beach. He'd do it. She could see it in his eyes. His way out of the engagement. But would he hold his tongue if he knew her secret? Perhaps, once he understood. . . She'd have to risk it.

She drew in a ragged breath. "I can't tell you, but I can show you. Tomorrow night."

eight

Melissa slipped out the door, waggling her fingers back at Sarah. "I've got my key. Don't wait up for me."

"You know I have to. I never rest easy until you're back, miss. And I'm worried, you taking *him*. What if he blows the whistle?"

"If I don't take him, he says he'll tell Father I'm meeting a man at night. I have no choice. Now, I must go. He's waiting."

She closed the door and stood still to allow her eyes to adjust to the darkness. An ever-present damp smell off the lake surrounded her.

Please, Lord, let him understand. I don't want to take him, but I don't know what else to do. If he does tell, help me to bear it. Help me to stand up to Father and Jonathan.

Her shoes crunched on the path. She slipped through the iron gate, latching it with a *click* that sounded like a gunshot to her ears. Melissa sucked in her bottom lip and melted into the hedge. No lights appeared in the upstairs windows.

He was waiting for her—but not alone.

"What is this?"

"A carriage. Surely you've heard of them? I'm sorry I don't have an automobile. I've one ordered, but it hasn't arrived yet."

"We can't have this standing in the street while we're inside. The Kennebrae crest on the door would be a dead giveaway."

She couldn't see his eyes under the brim of his hat, but his hand on her arm closed tight. "Use common sense for once. You'll ride in my carriage, or you won't go. Where do I tell the driver to take us?"

The obstinate man needed a kick in the shin. He was ruining everything, and he didn't even seem to care.

"The Cassell Building." With bad grace she climbed into

the carriage and plopped onto the seat.

He ducked inside and eased down on the seat opposite her. He put his gray-gloved hands atop his walking stick and stared at her. "Are you sure you just can't tell me what this is all about? I'd much rather be home in my own bed right now than traipsing about the harbor at this hour."

She lifted her chin and gave him a haughty stare in the light of the carriage lamps. "You can always let me out and go home. No one invited you. You're here of your own stubborn free will."

He laughed but not a friendly one. "Don't speak to me of stubborn willfulness. You epitomize the term. I can only imagine our destination. You say it isn't a clandestine meeting with a man, so I can only surmise the truth. A gambling den? Is that it? Are you squandering your inheritance on the turn of a card or the roll of a die? I've heard there are a few such establishments in the harbor area, though I confess I've never been to one."

"Don't be ridiculous. Of course I'm not gambling. I wouldn't begin to know how."

He grunted. The sound grated on Melissa like sour notes on the piano.

The carriage clattered to a stop. Jonathan opened the door and hopped out, then he held up his hand to help her alight.

Her feet had barely hit the pavement when she turned to him. "Please, won't you at least send the carriage away? No one could mistake it in this town, and it would cause talk. Please?"

"I don't intend to be here that long. The carriage stays. People will think I'm working late as we're right across the street from my own building."

She wanted to whack him with her handbag. Stubborn oaf. If only Peter and Wilson were here. He needed another crack on the head.

Tears of frustration stung her eyes. Before she completely embarrassed herself, she lifted her hem and headed around to the side of the multistoried brick building.

Narrow strips of light seeped around the edges of the basement windows. Thick bars covered the arched glass at street level. She descended the concrete steps to the basement entrance, her shoes echoing grittily.

Jonathan followed behind without a word.

She dug in her handbag for the key, but before she could use it, the door cracked open. She blinked in the light, the heat from inside the building puffing against her face.

"Melissa. We've been waiting." Beatrice Britten smiled at her, reaching for her hand to draw her inside. She glanced over Melissa's shoulder and froze, eyes wide.

"I'm sorry. He made me bring him." Guilt swamped Melissa, along with anger at Jonathan for putting her in this position. "This is Jonathan Kennebrae, my. . ." She swallowed hard. "My fiancé."

Beatrice narrowed her eyes, looking Jonathan over from shiny boots to brushed hair. "What do you want here? This isn't any place for the likes of you." She put her hand to her hip, bunching her apron over her plain wool dress.

"I'll be the judge of that." Jonathan didn't back down from her scrutiny or her unwelcoming glare.

"The rest of them aren't going to like it. I don't know that we should let him in. You know what will happen—"

"Please," Melissa interrupted, "I'll vouch for him."

Beatrice gave them both one more doubt-loaded glance before stepping back. Melissa hurried inside. Jonathan entered, removing his hat and smoothing his hair.

A narrow hallway with doors on one side, lit at long intervals with electric bulbs on cords from the ceiling, led off to the right. A rumble of voices came from the far end.

"Go ahead." Beatrice waved them down the hall. "I'm still waiting for folks."

Melissa eased off her gloves as she hurried toward the far end. Jonathan kept pace easily.

At the last door she turned to plead with him one more

time, but the determined look in his eyes and the set of his jaw told her it was no use. She opened the door.

❧

Jonathan steeled himself, but nothing prepared him for the scene that met his eyes.

All noise ceased. At least two dozen pairs of eyes stared at him. Women crammed every corner of the room.

Piles of fabric lay on tables in the center of the room, yellow, white, and purple. Around one small table near the door, six young women huddled with books and paper. A blackboard covered most of one wall, while pegs holding more fabric dominated another. What was this place?

"At least you now know I'm not meeting men here." Melissa crossed her arms and gave him a petulant glare. Her mouth scrunched up prettily, her thick lashes filtering her look.

For the first time he took in her dress. Plain in every respect. Dull brown tweed coat, ordinary black skirts showing below, and a simple straw boater with a black ribbon. She dressed like the other women in the room.

"What is this place? And what is the fabric for?"

"We're organizing a rally, and the fabric is for sashes and banners."

He didn't know whether to laugh or shout. "A rally? What's so secret about a rally? What cause could necessitate all this cloak-and-dagger nonsense?"

Every eye in the room was still on him, every ear listening.

"It's all right, ladies." Melissa sought to reassure them. "This is my fiancé, Mr. Jonathan Kennebrae."

At least this time she didn't choke on the term. He chose not to analyze how content he was to have her recognize him as her intended.

She grabbed his elbow and tugged him over to the blackboard. "It's a rally for women's suffrage. Now do you understand?"

He looked about the room again.

Though the women had gone back to their work, no one

was talking. They cast suspicious glances at him, particularly the group with the books in the corner.

"I'm afraid I must be obtuse. I fail to see the need to hide in a basement. The issue of women's suffrage is not a new one. Rallies for the enfranchisement of women have been held in many cities in this country."

Melissa closed her eyes and shook her head slowly, as if amazed at his denseness. "Not in this city and not with these women. Come here—maybe then you will understand." She led him to the corner table.

Wide eyes, pale hair, narrow bodies. The six women could be sisters.

"The women in this room are for the most part wives and daughters of dockworkers. They're immigrants, mostly from Scandinavia but Germany and the Slavic countries, too. We meet here at night because it is the only time many of these women are free of their other responsibilities. They sacrifice sleep to come here. And it isn't just for these women we're working. It's for women in every corner of this state. If certain people knew we were planning this rally, they would take steps to stop it. So we've kept it quiet."

"How many women are involved in this?"

"More than one hundred at last count. Obviously we can't all come every night. We take turns. And until now, no one has breathed a word of it outside the circle." Again the accusing look.

"All right." Jonathan crossed his arms, relieved her night ramblings were so benign. "But what about the books and the blackboard?"

"Some of these women barely speak English. We, the other educated ladies and myself, take turns teaching them to read and write. They want to speak and read English. They want to take part in the government of their new country, to be able to understand what their children are learning in school, to read the newspaper. They aren't stupid, like so many people think. They are intelligent, strong women who deserve a chance to speak for themselves in this country." Each word came more forcefully, her hands fisted, eyes flashing.

He rubbed his hand over the lower half of his face. The eyes of these women—worried, harried, tired—pierced him. How could he, who loved reading so much, who owed so much to his own schooling, deny them the chance to learn to read, to better themselves? As for women's suffrage, well, he had to admit, he'd not given it much thought.

"What are you going to do, Jonathan? I'm telling you right now, this movement will go on. It's too important. If you let the secret out, the meetings will just move to another place. It might slow us down, but we won't stop." Her cheeks were flushed, her eyes glowing with the passion of her cause. He had no idea she had such fire inside.

He cleared his throat, stepping back.

"Well, what are you going to do, Jonathan?" She challenged him again, hands on hips.

"I don't know. I'm going to think about it." And he'd have to do some hard thinking about how his attraction to her was growing. He tunneled his fingers through his hair.

She turned, tossing a glance at him over her shoulder. "Well, if you're staying, grab a needle and thread or a primer. We have work to do."

nine

"Stop your gloating." Jonathan pushed Grandfather's chair down the hallway toward Lawrence Brooke's office.

"Now, now, don't be cranky. You'd think you didn't sleep at all last night. Are you nervous?" Grandfather clasped his portfolio in his weathered hands. "It's a mere formality."

"I'm not signing anything today. I told you that. And if I could think of a way to delay this meeting, I would." Especially until he got his feelings for Melissa under control.

He hardly understood himself these days. Even after returning from seeing her home last night, he lay awake, hands behind his head, staring at the ceiling but seeing her face, hearing her voice as she patiently corrected pronunciation, smelling her rose perfume each time she came near.

"You're only putting off the inevitable. You'll see. It will be for the best."

A clerk stood at the end of the hall, holding the oak and glass door open. Jonathan nodded his thanks and directed the chair through the doorway.

Geoffrey met them first, his most impartial lawyer's expression firmly in place.

Lawrence Brooke sat behind a massive carved desk. An inkwell in the shape of a sinister black panther crouched on the glass top, looking ready to pounce on the unwary. Lawrence stood, grave faced. "Let's go into the conference room, shall we?"

Jonathan wheeled Grandfather through to an adjoining room. A long oval table dominated the space, surrounded by high-backed chairs. He nodded to Wasserman, not surprised to see his grandfather's favorite lawyer in attendance. At least Jonathan had Geoffrey there for moral support.

Two other occupants captured Jonathan's attention. Almina

Brooke sat at the head of the table as if to conduct the meeting herself. On her right, Melissa stared at her lap. He hadn't expected her to be here.

Melissa looked up, eyes pleading with him.

His heart jumped. She had pale gray smudges under each eye. A glare from her mother had her dropping her hand from her mouth to her lap. Jonathan was amazed at how familiar the gesture had become to him in such a short time. She always bit her nails when she was worried. A wave of protectiveness washed over him.

Jonathan strode the length of the table and took a seat beside her, ignoring the questioning look from Geoffrey and the triumphant gleam in Grandfather's eyes. No one seemed to appreciate how difficult this was, especially for Melissa. The two of them were being bartered like company assets.

He acknowledged Mrs. Brooke and listened while introductions were made. Lawrence Brooke's lawyers flanked him, while his secretary, a pale wraith of a man, sat along the wall taking notes. Wasserman sat beside Grandfather to guard his interests. Geoff sat between Jonathan and Grandfather.

Melissa put her hand on Jonathan's arm.

He bent low to hear her whisper, "Are you going to tell?"

For hours he had wrestled with this very question. If he spilled her secret, he was free. No engagement, no marriage, no merger. All he had to do was raise a fuss about her nightly jaunts, the suffrage politics, declare her unsuitable as his bride.

Lawrence Brooke had been outspoken on more than one occasion against giving women the franchise. Women—in his opinion, being the weaker sex—were unable to bear the responsibility of voting in political elections.

Grandfather would sputter and fume, but Jonathan would be free and still have Kennebrae Shipping, too. There was no way Grandfather would force him to marry a woman who was a political radical.

Jonathan shot a glance at Almina. By no stretch of the imagination could she be considered weak, but she would be mortified, humiliated if her daughter's character were called into question.

And what of Melissa herself? Could he ruin her reputation, bring down scandal and scorn on her just to extricate himself from the engagement? The thought of her wounded expression, the hurt he would cause her made him wince.

Not to mention the women associated with her in the cause. Those hardworking, immigrant women struggling to learn to read, to better themselves and fight for women's rights in a new country. Dreaming their new lives in America would be better than the oppression and poverty of their homelands. What right did he have to dash those dreams? Though he had never given much thought to women's suffrage, after seeing those women, seeing the passion Melissa had for them, he found he was inclined to support the idea.

He looked into Melissa's eyes, his heart hammering against his waistcoat. "No, your secret's safe with me." In that moment he knew he'd do whatever he could to keep her secret, to protect her in any way he could.

Relief flooded her face. For a moment he thought she might throw her arms around him and hug him. He tamped down his disappointment when she didn't. She returned her eyes to the mangled handkerchief in her lap.

He shifted in his chair. "I'm surprised to see you here."

"Mother insisted she had one item to discuss with me present. Then we would leave the rest to the men."

Jonathan nodded and sat back to endure the proceedings.

Attaché cases were opened, papers spread, and lawyers huddled, offering and counteroffering.

Jonathan listened with only half an ear, distracted by what Melissa's secret could mean for both of them and half curious as to what Almina Brooke felt was so important she needed to oversee that part of the contract herself. He wasn't left long to wonder.

"I have to insist"—Almira interrupted his thoughts—"that a certain amount of funds be settled on Melissa at her marriage by you, Lawrence, which shall be hers alone, to be used at her discretion."

Melissa looked up. Her hands tightened into fists.

Jonathan sat up, his attention totally caught. Every man at the table did likewise.

Lawrence cleared his throat and lowered his brows at his wife. "Almina? Are you suggesting Jonathan will not give our daughter a suitable allowance?"

All eyes swiveled to Jonathan to gauge his reaction. His chest prickled. "Mr. Brooke, I fully intend—" What did he intend? Certainly he wasn't entertaining the thought of actually going through with this marriage, was he?

Almina tapped her fingers on the table. "Lawrence, this isn't about Jonathan or allowances. I feel strongly that Melissa should have a nest egg of her own. You know, for those little things a woman needs. Or even to provide a special gift for her children's birthdays or her husband's. This money should come from us, from you, on her wedding day."

An uneasy feeling climbed Jonathan's rib cage. Almina was plotting his children? He darted a look at Melissa, whose cheeks glowed. He should say something, but what?

Lawrence mulled over his wife's words, tugging at his mustache.

The lawyers sat still, pens hovering.

"Very well. How much?"

"I should think two million would be suitable." Almina didn't bother to hide the challenge in her eyes.

Jonathan wasn't sure if he gasped, but he knew Geoffrey sucked in a breath. Two million for an opening salvo. The woman had courage.

She went on. "Given the sums involved, I should think two million dollars, to be used by Melissa as she sees fit, providing she marries Mr. Kennebrae, is not too much to ask. You're talking about a merger worth ten times that much. What you do with the rest of the marriage contract is up to you, but I insist that you do right by your daughter."

No one moved.

Grandfather's eyes shone like hot coals.

Almina stared at Lawrence.

He studied her for a long moment, her challenge to his

generosity hanging over the table like a sword. He pursed his lips. At last Lawrence reached forward and dipped his pen in an inkwell. "Make it three million, my wedding gift to Melissa."

Melissa stiffened and started to speak, but Almina's claw came down on her arm, squeezing it.

Jonathan frowned and took Melissa's other hand from her lap, closing his around it, surprised at her cold flesh.

Almina's triumphant look made him wonder if three million wasn't her aim all along. "Very good. That settled, Melissa and I will depart. Good day, gentlemen."

Jonathan released Melissa's hand.

When the ladies rose, every man did, too, save Grandfather.

Melissa gave Jonathan one last stunned look before following her dragon of a mother from the room.

≈

"That went well." Geoffrey tapped some files against his leg as they walked into the Kennebrae Shipping offices. "I had no idea Brooke was worth so much. A twenty-million-dollar wedding settlement, with an expected fifty-million-dollar inheritance. Not including a three-million-dollar nest egg for the bride apart from it all. It boggles the mind."

Jonathan grunted. "I didn't know Grandfather had branched out in so many areas." Admittedly Jonathan had focused his attention only on Kennebrae Shipping. To find that his family had interests in so many cities and in so many ventures astounded him.

A foundry in Cleveland. Rental properties in New York City, Boston, and Charleston. Shares in railroads, mines, and manufacturing. How many times during the meeting had Grandfather stared at Jonathan when Brooke mentioned grain contracts and new ships?

Jonathan opened his office door and stopped. Geoffrey bumped into his back.

"Thought you'd never get here. Where've you been, and where's Grandfather?" Noah lounged in Jonathan's chair, his boots propped up on the blotter. He twirled a peaked cap on one finger.

"Noah! You weren't expected for two more days. When did you get in?" Jonathan's gaze flew to the windows. Sure enough, the *Bethany* sat at the Number One Dock.

"Midmorning. The repairs weren't as extensive as first thought. They patched the leak temporarily, and we limped on home. I figured it would be better to have the majority of the work done here where our own shipbuilders can oversee the repairs. And I want the entire boiler gone over. That will take two or three weeks. Then I figure I can squeeze in one more trip through the Soo before we're iced in for winter." He swept his boots off the desk and stood.

Jonathan grabbed him in a hug. The smell of open water, windy skies, and coal smoke lingered in Noah's thick wool tunic. "When did you get so strong?"

Noah laughed. "A life on the water builds muscles. More than shuffling papers behind a desk." He rubbed his chin. "What do you think of the beard?"

Jonathan studied the bushy brown whiskers covering his brother's face. "Is that what you're calling that weed patch?"

Noah laughed and cuffed Jonathan on the shoulder. "All captains wear beards. It's a mark of authority." He turned to Geoffrey. "Hello, Geoff. Still minding Kennebrae's interests?"

Geoff grinned and shook Noah's hand. "Today more than usual, Noah. Welcome home."

Noah settled into a chair before the fireplace. "Is that where you were? Some stuffy meeting?"

Jonathan squared up the piles of paper on his desk. "Yes. And, Noah, we need to talk. Grandfather has been up to his old tricks, only this time it's worse."

"You know, sometimes I'm afraid to pull into the harbor. What's he done now?"

"Geoff, have a seat. You can clarify any points I miss." Jonathan leaned his elbows on the desk and steepled his fingers. When his lawyer was seated, Jonathan began a recounting of recent events.

"And so," he finished up, "I have to get married or forfeit Kennebrae Shipping altogether."

Noah sat, slack jawed as a sturgeon. "Are you serious?"

"Dead serious. We were just at a meeting with Brooke's lawyers to draw up the contract."

"You're not going through with it? Isn't there some way to stop it?"

Jonathan shook his head. "Not that I'm prepared to take at this time. Geoff, show him the paperwork."

Geoff dug in his file and produced a thick document.

Noah perused only the first page. "Did you sign this?" He looked at Jonathan with grave eyes.

"No, I told them I wouldn't sign anything today, and I didn't expect them to either. Each side needs a few days at least to go over the transaction. Hopefully that will give me time to find a way out without losing Kennebrae Shipping." *And without sullying Melissa's reputation.*

"But you said the engagement had already been announced. If you back out now, folks might think there's something wrong with the girl. Is there something wrong with her?"

"Not a thing." Heat crept up Jonathan's cheeks at the vehemence of his reply.

Noah sat back and studied Jonathan. A slow grin spread over Noah's face. "You like her. That's why you haven't told Grandfather what he can do with Kennebrae Shipping. You don't want to get out of this engagement."

"Don't be ridiculous. I barely know her."

"Well, what's she like?" Noah tossed the papers back to Geoff. "No, on second thought, you can't be unbiased. I'd rather hear it from Geoffrey. You've met her, haven't you, Geoff?"

Jonathan thrust his chair back and strode to the windows. Noah could be such a tease. He'd forgotten how his younger brothers could grate on him at times.

"She's beautiful." Geoffrey jumped in. "Lovely blue eyes, brown hair. I hear she plays the piano and speaks French fluently. Jonathan took me along to the luncheon where the engagement was announced." Jonathan could hear the grin in Geoff's voice and tightened his jaw.

"Grandfather's working fast. Go on, Geoff."

Jonathan groaned and hung his head. Noah was bound to hear it sometime, but Jonathan had hoped he'd be far away when his brother got the story. But perhaps it was better to get it over with now. He turned and sent a glare Geoffrey's way, knowing it wouldn't stop his lawyer from telling the tale with relish.

"Lawrence Brooke announced the engagement, and the bride-to-be jumped up, squawked a little at Jonathan, then fainted dead away." Geoff glanced guiltily in Jonathan's direction but not before Jonathan saw the amusement there, too.

Noah began to laugh. "So you're saying the thought of marrying big brother knocked her out cold?"

"He swept her off her feet."

Both men doubled over, howling.

Jonathan fisted his hands and envisioned popping both of them on their noses.

When Noah composed himself, he sat up, eyes full of mischief. "I've got to meet this girl. You'll give me an introduction, right? And I know just what to get you for an engagement present."

"What?"

"Smelling salts!"

Little brothers could be such pains. Time for some revenge.

"Noah, there's more."

"What, did she have a fit of hysteria when a wedding date was set?" He couldn't stop chuckling.

"I'm not the only one Grandfather is hustling down the aisle."

Noah quit laughing. He regarded Jonathan with a wary eye.

"He's got brides all picked out for you and Eli, too."

Noah sagged into his chair, the wind taken out of his sails.

Satisfaction settled in Jonathan's chest. Perhaps now Noah would be serious and find a way out of this mess for all of them.

"Okay, this is beyond funny now." Noah swallowed hard.

ten

Melissa stood on the low table, arms out to her sides at shoulder height, trying not to move. Pinpricks threatened with each breath.

Mother and the seamstress she'd imported from New York huddled a few feet away, tossing looks over their shoulders and murmuring.

"It's so beautiful. I wish I was getting married." Her friend Zylphia wound some lace trim around her hand. "You look like a princess."

I feel like a dress-up doll. Mother's doll to dress up and show off when it suits her. Melissa forced a smile and kept her thoughts to herself. It did her little good to voice them.

"The train should be at least ten feet long. And trim it with the seed pearls." Mother lifted a handful of the opalescent beads, letting them dribble through her fingers back into the bowl.

The seamstress, a petite, dark Frenchwoman, took notes and nodded, keeping her lips pinched tight. Perhaps the habit of holding pins in her mouth had left it permanently scrunched.

"And use these crystals, too. In the floral pattern we discussed. Recreate the pattern in this lace." Mother plucked the lace from Zylphia's hand and unrolled it.

The skein landed with a thump on the rug. Zylphia rolled her eyes and shrugged, and Melissa stifled a giggle. Not more than two minutes ago Mother had insisted Zylphia roll up the excess lace to prevent its getting damaged.

Madame Lisette began removing the pins from the cotton mock-up pieces draped all over Melissa's frame.

With relief Melissa lowered her arms and stepped out of the skirt. Sarah held her dressing gown, and Melissa slipped her arms into the comforting garment. Her chemise and petticoats were no protection against the chill in the attic sewing room.

"Get dressed, Melissa, and you and Zylphia can take tea." Mother looked up from leafing through sketches. "I'll be here quite some time yet. I still can't decide if this new charmeuse fabric is the best choice or not."

Melissa hurried to her room and slipped into a yellow dress. Her hair looked a mess from pulling garments over her head. Unpinned it fell to her waist in heavy brown curls. She plaited it, her fingers quick from long practice, and left the braid hanging down her back.

The usual sense of calm Melissa experienced when entering the blue parlor failed to come over her. As always, her mother's forceful personality drove the wedding plans, drowning the household in a storm surge of details about fabric, music, flowers, attendants. And she consulted Melissa not at all. A piece of driftwood had about as much say in its destination.

Zylphia was seated on one of the velvet chairs, leafing through a photo album.

Melissa forswore being ladylike and flopped down on the ivory damask couch, plopping her feet up on a cushion.

"Well?" Zylphia pounced on her, grabbing her shoulders and giving her a little shake. "Are you going to tell me? You promised."

"Let's get through tea, and I'll tell all."

Anne, the parlor maid, entered with the tea tray, her black skirts swishing. She set the tray down on the marble-topped table. "Can I get you anything else?"

Melissa shook her head. "Thank you, Anne. That will be all. Why don't you go put your feet up for a few minutes?"

"Thank you, miss." She bobbed her head and left the parlor, her heels clicking on the parquet.

"Tell me. I can't stand it anymore." Zylphia poured her tea and stirred in a spoonful of sugar. "What's so urgent?"

Melissa regretted her rash promise to tell Zylphia her secret, but she desperately needed someone to confide in. And Zylphia could be a help if she would. The more women they had, the better. "You have to promise not to tell anyone. Not your mother, not your maid, no one."

"I promise. Now tell me."

Melissa sat up and checked that the door was closed. Then she leaned close to Zylphia. "I'm involved in underground meetings to organize a women's suffrage rally here in Duluth."

Zylphia sat back, disbelief spread over her pretty face. "Women's suffrage? Is that all? I thought it was something romantic or dangerous."

"It is, dangerous at least. Why else would I sneak out in the middle of the night and walk downtown for the meetings? And could you imagine what my father would say if he found out?"

"You sneak out at night?" Zylphia's eyes lit up. She leaned forward. "Tell me more."

Melissa described her nighttime activities, mentioning how Peter and Wilson picked her up in their family delivery wagon and watched over her to see that she came to no harm. About the women who wanted to learn to read and write, and who most of all wanted to vote, to have a say in the government that ruled them. "And there's more. Jonathan knows."

"He does? And he doesn't mind?" Zylphia's mouth opened in surprise.

"I don't think he's very happy about it, but so far he hasn't told anyone. He followed me down there. The first time he didn't make it to the building. Peter and Wilson got a little overeager and knocked him on the head. That's why he had the bruise on his temple at the sailing luncheon."

Zylphia squeezed her hands together. "What happened?"

"He was angry. I had to tell him about the meetings, or he was going straight to Father. That would've been disastrous. Father doesn't know anything about it, and I'd like to keep it that way. I took Jonathan to one of the meetings, hoping that once he saw the women and how much they were being helped and how serious we are about this, he might relent and keep quiet. I think it might have worked." Melissa picked up the teapot. "Anyway he stayed for the whole three hours and even listened to some of the ladies who were learning to read."

"He listened to lessons?"

Warmth tickled Melissa's heart. He'd sat at the table with those Norwegian ladies listening to their halting English, his long legs cramped under the rickety chair, his hair falling on his forehead. He hadn't laughed at them or belittled their lack of education, nor had he sneered at the banners and sashes, the pamphlets and placards piled about the room. "I don't know what his next move will be. I haven't even seen him since the lawyer's meeting on Monday."

"Did your father really give you three million dollars?"

Melissa twisted her mouth in a grimace. "Not exactly. None of the papers has been signed yet. If and when I marry Jonathan Kennebrae, I will receive three million dollars of my own money."

"And Jonathan agreed? No woman has money that isn't her husband's to control."

"I will, thanks to Mother's insistence."

"What are you going to do with it?"

"I don't know. I have a few ideas."

A knock sounded at the door. The housekeeper marched in, her keys jangling on the chatelaine at her waist. "A note arrived for you, Miss Brooke."

Mrs. Trolley's sallow face pinched in displeasure. She held out an envelope, wrinkled and smudged. "The man who delivered it looked rather. . .untidy."

Melissa's lips twitched at this, the most dire description one could earn from Mrs. Trolley. "Thank you."

Mrs. Trolley looked down her hooked nose, swept the tea tray with a glance, and departed.

"Who's it from?"

Melissa slit the envelope with a butter knife. She scanned

the single sheet of paper. Her mind raced. "What are we going to do?"

"What?" Zylphia's voice rose in alarm. "What is it?"

Melissa bit her thumbnail, trying and tossing out ideas. No, that wouldn't work. No, no, no. Why now? She folded the paper and slipped it into her pocket. "I need some help. I've got to see Jonathan."

❧

Jonathan slung the papers down on his desk and rubbed his palm across the back of his neck. Why couldn't he concentrate?

Melissa. Plain and simple, she wouldn't leave his head. Even Noah had noticed his lack of concentration, his gazing into nothing, his preoccupation. Thoughts of her invaded every waking moment and even his dreams. He imagined he could smell her rose perfume, hear her laughter, see her determined little face as she stood up to him for what she believed in.

Her note crackled in his pocket, and he withdrew it. What kind of sap was he that even the sight of her handwriting stirred him? She needed to see him, as soon as possible.

He'd fired off a reply inviting her and her parents to dinner so quickly he'd smeared the ink. It pleased him that she needed him. The protective feelings he'd begun to harbor toward her swelled.

Jonathan paced his sitting room, his feet quiet on the Persian rug. He muttered to himself, sifting through his feelings, analyzing, evaluating, testing each one.

"Why are you so distracted by her? Sure, she's pretty, but there has to be more."

He stopped before the windows, pulling the drapes aside to look down on the pewter surface of the lake.

"Is it the money?" He had to face the question squarely.

An honest search of his heart told him the truth. No, his feelings had nothing to do with money.

"I'd feel this way if she had no more money in this world than those immigrant women she tutors." A rush of relief followed the statement. He paused, gripping the heavy brocade fabric.

"But what is it I feel?"

Protective. He could acknowledge that. Friendly? No, it was more than that. He had plenty of friends, and he'd never felt this way about any of them.

"Are you really as dense as that?"

The unexpected voice caused Jonathan to spin toward the door.

Noah leaned against his door frame, ankles and arms crossed.

"How long have you been there?" Jonathan scowled, shoving his hands into his pockets.

"Long enough to know what you're too dumb to see."

"And what might that be?" Jonathan pursed his lips.

Noah rolled his eyes. "You're in love with the girl you're supposed to marry."

Jonathan tensed. "Don't be ridiculous."

"You're the one who's being ridiculous. It's as plain as a lighthouse beacon on a clear night that you love her. You've been all but walking into walls this week. You swing from wanting to talk about her all the time to not wanting to talk about her at all. You've lost your perspective and your sense of humor. If you don't love her, then you're giving a mighty good imitation."

Did he love her? How could he tell? All he knew was that he felt better when he was with her than he'd ever felt before, and when they weren't together, she was all he could think about. Maybe he did love her.

Noah crossed the room and put his hand on Jonathan's shoulder. "It's not a crime to be happy, Jonathan. If you love her, then try to win her heart. It will be worth it in the end."

Jonathan nodded slowly, his mind whirling. In love with Melissa Brooke? Wouldn't that beat all?

eleven

The carriage rocked along the street in and out of pools of light cast by the street lamps. Melissa smoothed her skirts and tugged at her gloves. Sarah had done a wonderful job getting Melissa ready on such short notice.

The tone of the horses' hooves changed as they pulled off the road and onto a gravel drive. The carriage lurched to a stop. She didn't know if she'd feel better or worse if her parents had been able to accompany her. But they'd had a previous engagement. It had taken all of Melissa's persuasive powers to get her mother to allow her to accept Jonathan's invitation to dinner at Kennebrae House without her parents.

The driver helped her alight. Lamps burned on either side of the massive front doors, casting shadows under the domed roof of the porte cochere. Before she could ring the bell, the door swung open.

A silver-haired man in a black suit stepped back for her to enter. "Good evening, Miss Brooke." He inclined his head.

She hoped her smile wasn't as nervous as her quivering middle. What was the matter with her?

"May I take your cloak, miss?" His gloved hands gleamed white in the light of the chandelier.

She loosened the velvet ties at her throat, trying to swallow. The reception hall stretched at least fifty feet to the right and left. Broad steps to the second floor dominated the wall across from her, everything paneled in darkly stained oak. Oaken carved pillars stood sentinel at intervals, vines and leaves and flowers with the occasional cupid face peeking out. She'd heard about the fantastic parties held in this room in years past, but nothing had prepared her for the sheer size of the building. It was less a home than a castle. Every inch declared it the abode of men. No flowers or bright colors, nothing soft or gentle.

The butler took her wrap and draped it over his arm. "This way, if you please." He led her to the left, nearly to the end of the long hall before stopping at a door. "The gentlemen are in the parlor." He opened the door. "Miss Brooke, sir."

When he stepped aside, Melissa entered the room. A fire blazed in the marble fireplace. Another chandelier gleamed overhead, throwing prisms of light on the painted ceiling.

"Melissa." Jonathan came forward to greet her.

She put out her hand. "Thank you for the dinner invitation. I need to speak with you."

"And I with you, but later." Jonathan tucked her hand into his elbow and led her to the fireplace. "Grandfather, Melissa's here."

"Hello, my dear. You're looking splendid. Come, sit down. Dinner will be ready in a few minutes. Warm yourself." He patted the chair beside him. "I'm delighted you could join us. It's too bad your parents couldn't come, but we'll have them over soon."

Melissa eased into the chair, trying to calm her nerves.

Abraham Kennebrae was as charming as ever, chattering away.

Jonathan stood by the mantel, looking down on her. His intent gaze heated her through more than the fire. Though she'd thought of him constantly for days, being in the same room with him made her heart skip and her breath come fast.

The door opened once more. A bearded man of Jonathan's height sauntered in, hands in his pockets. He stopped when he saw Melissa. "Well, this is a pleasant surprise. It's been years since this parlor was graced with so beautiful a woman. I'm Noah Kennebrae."

He took Melissa's offered hand and bent over it gallantly, squeezing her fingers and kissing the air above her knuckles. "You must be the girl who stole Jonathan's heart. He's been walking around like a lovesick duck for the last week." Noah grinned wickedly at his brother. "But even his description of you doesn't do you justice."

Jonathan had been talking about her? Did he think she was pretty? Melissa tried to squelch that vain thought, but it wouldn't lie down. She'd been on his mind. Was his brother's teasing true? Had she stolen his heart? Ridiculous, not when he wanted out of this engagement as badly as she did. And she did want out, didn't she?

Jonathan's brows shot down, and he glared at his brother.

Noah chuckled, his teeth white against his dark beard.

Jonathan took two steps and removed Melissa's hand from Noah's grasp. "Knock it off, Noah." His tone brooked no argument.

Melissa clasped her hands in her lap, glancing from one man to the other.

Noah didn't seem upset by Jonathan's glower. On the contrary, his grin widened, and he shoved his hands back into his pockets under his coat and rocked on his heels.

Abraham's eyes danced, a smile quivering about his lips. "Ah, this is just what I envisioned when this engagement was first spoken of. The banter of family, the softness of a woman's presence in our masculine household. If only Eli could be here to share it with us."

Melissa turned her attention away from Jonathan to his grandfather. "Eli?"

"Eli is the youngest of the Kennebrae brothers, though only by a few minutes. He and Noah are twins, similar but not identical. He's in Virginia studying shipbuilding. He'll be home in a few months."

Jonathan took a seat on the settee, stretching his long legs toward the fire.

Noah leaned against the wall beside the fireplace. "And some news he'll come home to. If I were him, I'd stay away for a long time."

Abraham's hands fisted. "We've been through this." His

voice, so sharp in contrast to just minutes ago, startled Melissa. "He will accede to my wishes, or he'll suffer the consequences, as will you all. I'm still the head of this family." Pink suffused his pale cheeks.

Melissa looked to Jonathan, wondering how he would take this ultimatum.

He sat up, placed his elbows on his knees, and stared into the flames. Tired lines creased his face, the barest hint of bruise still coloring his temple. "Yes, Grandfather, we know. You've made it abundantly clear on more than one occasion."

"Don't get smart with me, young man. And don't patronize me." Abraham's breath rasped, his narrow chest rising and falling quickly. "And don't think I don't know what you're up to with delaying signing the marriage contract. Mark my words, this marriage will proceed."

"Take it easy. You know the doctor says you shouldn't get worked up," Noah said, standing up straight. "And you're forgetting our guest. Melissa, don't mind them."

Apprehension fluttered across her skin. Was she to be a bone of contention between them always?

Abraham's head swiveled Melissa's way, the heat dying out of his face. "I beg your pardon, my dear. You see, this is what comes of an all-male household. We quite forget our manners."

The butler stood in the doorway. "Dinner is served."

Jonathan wiped his hand down his face and rose as if burdened with a great weight, his jaw firm, the skin drawn tight over his cheekbones. He offered Melissa his arm.

She tucked her hand into his elbow while Noah took the handle of Abraham's chair and wheeled him ahead. Melissa's heart went out to Jonathan, battling his stubborn grandfather. She knew what it was to fight her own parents for a bit of freedom, a bit of individuality.

When she squeezed his arm, he looked down at her in surprise, causing heat to rush up her cheeks. She averted her gaze, swallowing hard. They walked in silence down the long, carpeted reception hall to the dining room at the other end of the house.

Silver candelabras graced the table, throwing light toward the gleaming gilded panels of the coffered ceiling. Rich, tooled leather covered the upper walls, a luxurious forest green.

Noah wheeled Abraham to the far end of the table under the portraits.

Jonathan led Melissa down the row of chairs and pulled out the one on Abraham's left. Jonathan took the chair opposite Melissa, with Noah on his right.

Abraham held out his hand to Melissa. Confused she placed her hand in his. The men all clasped hands and bowed their heads.

"Jonathan, will you offer the grace, please?" Abraham's voice cracked, and he cleared his throat.

Jonathan's voice comforted Melissa. He prayed, not by rote but as if he talked to a friend of long-standing, asking God's blessing on the food and those who partook of it and for a special blessing on Eli, so far from home. When he said, "Amen," Melissa looked up, catching his eye. Some of her butterflies concerning the reason for her coming tonight subsided. If he could talk to God like that, surely he would listen to her needs. But when could they be alone?

Two maids carried in the first course. Did they dine like this every night, or was this a special occasion because she was here?

Melissa and her mother often ate together in the evening. Lawrence Brooke spent long hours at his office or closeted away in his den working. He usually had a tray sent in about nine every night. Only when guests were expected did he break with his routine and dress for a formal dinner.

"The *Bethany* should be ready to pull out just after Thanksgiving. We can make one last dash to Chicago with ore and hustle back with a load of coal before the season ends." Noah picked up his fork.

Melissa studied Jonathan's younger brother. He had lines at the corners of his eyes, as if he spent a great deal of time looking out at the sun on the water. His hands were rough, calloused, and large, dwarfing his crystal water goblet. Sky blue eyes—so different from Jonathan's dark brown—didn't miss a trick. His mouth had the look of one with a sense of humor.

"That's leaving a bit late, don't you think? The weather's a bit tricky that time of year. You might be iced in by mid-November." Jonathan pursed his lips.

"Life's no fun if you don't take some risks. Anyway, I thought you wanted me to take another look at the docks in Chicago. Wasn't Jacobson headed down there to negotiate the sale?"

"What's this?" Abraham scowled. "I haven't heard about any docks in Chicago. When did this happen?"

"At the last board meeting. You weren't there, remember? You were holed up with your cronies, mapping out the future to suit yourself." Jonathan dropped his fork to his plate. "Like you have been for the last five board meetings. You said to take care of things myself, and that's just what I've done."

Abraham thumped the table with his fist. "I'm tired of this conversation. I've been over my reasons. Enough."

Melissa's skin prickled. How often this evening would she be reminded that she was a bartered bride? The food stuck in her throat, tasting of damp newspaper.

Jonathan flexed his jaw, clamping it shut on whatever he had been about to say.

Noah, his eyes filled with pity enough to make her squirm, changed the subject. "Melissa, I noticed you looking at the portraits." He waved toward the paintings in their heavy, gilded frames. "Those are our parents, Isaiah and Isabelle Kennebrae."

Melissa studied them, noting the dark hair Isaiah had passed on to his sons. Isabelle was more pleasant of feature than outright beautiful, but there was something in her expression, a liveliness, a fire, that drew Melissa's attention. She had yet to meet Eli, but both Jonathan and Noah had inherited that same passion—Jonathan for business and Noah for sailing. She made the appropriate comments and fell silent.

Dinner finished, as uncomfortable and strained as it had begun, Jonathan brooding and quiet, Abraham fuming, and Noah trying to carry the conversation. Melissa regretted coming tonight. If she married Jonathan, was this the evening entertainment she could look forward to for the rest of her life? If Noah hadn't been there, the meal would've been conducted in complete silence. Her dinner sat in her middle like an anchor.

twelve

"Why don't we go to the music room? Melissa can play for us." Abraham tossed his napkin on the table, breaking his silence. "We've got a Steinway. Hasn't been played since my wife died."

Melissa shot Jonathan a pleading look.

Jonathan held her chair for her as she rose.

"I must speak with you." She kept her voice low, tucking her hand into his offered elbow.

He nodded. "Later."

She stopped, tugging on his arm. "Not later. Now."

Noah halted pushing Abraham's chair for only a second, and she realized she'd spoken louder than she'd intended.

"We'll join you in a few moments." Jonathan slid her chair under the table and waited.

"We're not competing in a race," Abraham scolded. "Slow down." Noah's reply was muffled by the doors closing.

Jonathan and Melissa stood alone in the dining room. She stepped back a pace and crossed her arms at her waist, pressing against her middle to still her nerves.

His brooding expression softened. "I'm sorry about tonight. I haven't been a very good host. Sometimes an afternoon of butting heads with Grandfather leaves me in a black mood. You had something you wanted to say?"

The enormity of what she was asking hit her. What if he wouldn't help her? Where could she turn next? Could she trust him with this? *Lord, give me courage.*

"I. . .I need your help. And I haven't much time. I got a note from the night watchman at the Cassell Building. He's leaving for St. Paul tomorrow and won't be back for several months. Tonight is his last night."

He frowned in confusion. "I fail to see how this concerns

me. Surely they can find another night watchman."

"Of course they can." Was Jonathan being deliberately obtuse? "But the new watchman will hardly be likely to allow several immigrant ladies and dockworkers' wives into the building in the middle of the night. He'd drive them off or, worse, try to have them arrested for trespassing. The girls must clear the room out tonight."

Jonathan gripped the back of the carved mahogany chair, studying her. "What is it you are asking of me?"

She swallowed and wet her lips. His eyes fixed on her mouth, and a curious swirl started in her stomach. "We need another place to meet, and we need it tonight. Someplace safe."

He took a step toward her, towering over her, his gaze intent. "And did you have a place in mind?"

She nodded. He smelled of soap and spice. Her breath caught in her throat. What was he doing?

"Are you going to tell me?" His voice deepened, brushing across her like a caress.

She blinked in response and tried to remember what they were talking about. "Um. . .yes. The shipping office."

He raised an eyebrow. "You want to meet at Kennebrae Shipping? My office?" He went very still, and for a moment she thought he was going to refuse. Then he smiled, a slow, easy smile. "A good idea." He was so close she could feel his warmth through his dinner jacket. He raised his hands to caress her upper arms.

She shivered. "You are not yourself this evening, Jonathan. I expected. . ." She licked her lips again. "I thought you would be resistant to the idea."

His lips twitched. "You're right. I'm not myself. I'm tired. I'm tired to death of arguing with Grandfather." He bent a little closer. "I'm tired of wrestling with contracts, board members, and accountants' columns."

A few inches nearer, until he was only a breath away. "But most of all, I'm tired of fighting the urge to do this." He bent his head and kissed her, soft and incredibly gentle.

Her eyes fluttered closed, her heart beating so hard she thought he might feel it against his chest.

His hand came up to touch her throat, his thumb grazing her jaw. He stepped back, his eyes dark with feeling.

Her hand flew to her tingling lips. She swallowed hard and blinked, catching her breath.

"You're welcome to use the Kennebrae offices. In fact, use the private conference room connected to my office. You can haul your banners and books there, and I'll see no one disturbs them. The furnishings are much more comfortable than that basement storeroom you've been using. In fact, I'll send McKay to unlock the building and help the ladies move. He'll keep your secret safe. He's been harboring Kennebrae secrets for twenty years." Jonathan dug in his pocket and withdrew a key. "Here, take this. Then you can come and go as you please."

She didn't know which overwhelmed her more, his generosity or his kiss. She smiled inwardly. Definitely his kiss.

Gather your wits, girl. Don't let him see how it affected you.

"What's changed your mind? I expected you to be thrilled at our predicament. I'd have to stop going out at night if we had no place to meet."

"You seem to have caught me when my resistance was low . . .in several areas." He pressed the key into her hand. "Perhaps I take solace in knowing you will be safely tucked away in my offices, in comfort, instead of in that drafty, dank basement. Or perhaps I believe in your cause and want to help you all I can."

She narrowed her eyes, appraising his sincerity. "I'd like to believe that."

"Then do. Let's join Grandfather in the music room. I have a sudden desire to hear a nocturne." He led her down the hall, and she wasn't sure her feet even touched the pale blue carpeting.

The Steinway was beautiful with hand-carved legs like seated griffins in cherry, inlay marquetry in tendrils and leaves along the case, gleaming ivory keys, and a scrollwork music stand. But most beautiful of all, on the fallboard above the keys where the maker's name and city were usually displayed, this piano had a painting. A schooner in full sail, the rising sun picking out the details of masts and lines and rails, rode the waves of an aquamarine sea. Clouds in golds, pinks, and purples graced the sky. It was the most beautiful instrument she'd ever seen. She squelched the guilt she felt at not helping the ladies move tonight, salving her conscience that McKay would go in her stead.

She chose Beethoven's Moonlight Sonata. The music wrapped around her, carrying her away like the schooner on the melody and Jonathan's kiss.

thirteen

"You look different." Zylphia sipped her cup of chocolate, her eyes scanning the other diners. "Things must've gone well last night."

Melissa smiled and lowered her lashes. Last night. Her first kiss. She pressed her hand to her chest, feeling the key on a chain under her dress. The key to Kennebrae Shipping. The key to his heart?

"Things went wonderfully last night. At first it was a little rocky. Jonathan and his grandfather had been arguing, and dinner was a bit sticky, but the evening got much better after that."

"So tell me." Zylphia leaned toward her, squeezing her arm.

"They have a beautiful piano. I played Beethoven."

Her friend sagged back in her chair and rolled her eyes. "Oh phooey. I despair of you. I thought maybe something romantic had happened."

Melissa couldn't quell her smile.

Zylphia pounced. "I knew it. You are all lit up inside. Something must've happened."

"Jonathan agreed to let us—the cause, I mean—move into his office at night. Without any fuss at all. He sent a man to move the books and materials from the basement room across the street to his own conference room. We can work in comfort and safety, and he said we could use it as long as we like."

Zylphia blinked. "That's wonderful, but is that all?"

"It's all you're going to get from me." Melissa gave her a saucy grin. "Finish your chocolate. We've got shopping to do. I'm buying my trousseau, you know."

"Whatever happened, it must've been pretty nice. Yesterday

90

you couldn't be bothered to even look at the drawings for your wedding gown, and today we're buying linens and picking out silver."

"Speaking of picking out silver, we have an appointment in ten minutes at the jeweler's. Mother selected three patterns she thought might be suitable. I'm to choose the one I like best."

"At least she gave you that much leeway. You'd think it was her getting married, not you. She's planned everything from the music to the menu to the flowers."

Melissa shook her head. "At least she has good taste. And I don't care, as long as I'm marrying Jonathan."

Zylphia's cup rattled in the saucer. "That's it! That's what's different about you."

"What?"

"You're in love. You're in love with Jonathan Kennebrae."

Melissa laughed, joy bubbling up at hearing someone say the words her heart had been singing since that kiss last night. "You make it sound horrible. What's so wrong with being in love with the man I'm going to marry?"

"But you were totally against it yesterday. You said you were embarrassed to be a bartered bride, married only for your money and your name."

"Well, I was wrong. Jonathan is rich. He doesn't need my money. If you had seen the inside of Kennebrae House, you'd know how ridiculous the idea was. All that place needs is a woman's touch. And he cares about me. I know it. He trusts me. He even gave me the key to his building."

"How romantic." Zylphia's voice dripped with sarcasm. "Almost as good as sending flowers or writing poetry. You get free run of his office."

A little gloss went off the moment for Melissa, but she lifted her chin. "Well, he didn't have to be so generous. And he does care about me. He's been nothing but nice to me."

Zylphia shrugged. "Maybe you're right. I hope you are. Let's go spend some of your father's money."

Hours later they entered Castlebrooke's foyer, arm in arm, chilled from the raw November breeze coming in off Lake Superior. The footmen carried in their parcels, and Sarah helped them with their coats and hats.

"Sarah, will you have Mrs. Trolley send tea to the parlor? I'm frozen through." Melissa checked her reflection in the hall mirror and motioned to Zylphia. "Come. We've worked hard and deserve to put our feet up. If I never see another china or flatware pattern again, it will be too soon."

Before Zylphia could answer, Mother bustled into the foyer, a hectic look in her eyes. "Melissa, where have you been?"

Melissa stopped short in surprise. "I've been downtown, the jeweler's, the stationer's, the florist's."

"Well, there's no time for that. Jonathan's here, and he's been waiting almost an hour." Mother tugged on Melissa's hand. "Hurry up. Don't dawdle. I've been trying to make small talk, but he just keeps pacing the rug."

Happiness welled up inside Melissa, and she hurried to the parlor doors without a backward glance. Jonathan was here? Was he as eager to see her as she was to see him?

She opened the door, and he stopped in midstride. "Jonathan, I'm so sorry you had to wait."

He crossed the room and took her hands in his. Heat seared her cold fingers. "I needed to see you right away."

"Is something wrong?" Her thoughts raced. Would they not be able to use the conference room for their meetings? Had something gone awry with the transferring of the supplies? She knew she should've overseen it herself, but no, she let herself be talked into staying late and playing the Kennebrae piano.

"Yes." His brown eyes were grave, his face solemn. "I'm afraid I've committed a serious error."

She blinked and stepped back, withdrawing her hands. An error?

He put a hand into his pocket. "Yes, a serious social error."

Her mouth went dry. What could it be? Did he regret kissing her?

"I've blundered badly, but I intend to make it up to you now. It seems we've been planning a wedding, but you've been cheated out of a proper proposal." He dropped to one knee and reclaimed her hand. "Melissa Brooke, will you marry me?"

Time stopped for a moment when she stared into his eyes. Then happy tears pricked her eyelids, and she put her free hand up to cover her lips. No words would come. She could only nod.

He grinned, so handsome and confident, and opened his palm. On it lay a sapphire and diamond ring. He slid it on her finger and stood, opening his arms to her.

She went into his embrace, wrapping her arms around his neck and lifting her lips to his kiss. It was everything she remembered and better. She wanted it to go on forever.

A small cough brought her to her senses. They parted reluctantly to see Mother and Zylphia standing in the doorway. Mother wore a satisfied expression, and Zylphia had her hands clasped under her chin. She let out a sigh. "That was perfect."

❧

Melissa sat beside Jonathan on the settee, listening to Mother prattle on about the wedding plans. Melissa didn't care about the music, the flowers, the choral pieces. All she cared about was that Jonathan loved her and wanted to marry her. How silly that they'd both resisted so strongly at first.

God, You are good. You work out Your plans—the ones You know are best for us—even though we might resist at first. You do know the plans You have for us. Plans of hope and a future. Thank You for Jonathan. Thank You for bringing me someone who cares for me, who is interested in my causes. I'm sorry for doubting You and Your goodness.

She adjusted the ring on her finger, its clasp unfamiliar and heavy.

Zylphia could not contain her sighs, looking all dewy and romantic every time Melissa caught her eye.

Well, it was romantic. Melissa smiled and checked her finger again to make sure she wasn't dreaming. Zylphia was right. It was perfect.

"I couldn't be happier with how things are working out." Mother offered a plate of tea sandwiches to Zylphia but kept her eyes on Jonathan. "And did you bring the papers with you?"

A prickle of irritation skipped up Melissa's spine. Why did Mother have to bring up that stupid contract? Wasn't it enough that they cared for each other? They were blessed to be marrying for love not money, no matter how much of it each family had. With his kiss still a vivid memory, she no longer felt like a bartered bride.

"They're on the table, all signed and notarized."

"Good." Mother had that cat-who-ate-the-cream look of utter satisfaction with herself and her plans. "Things are moving along nicely."

fourteen

"Things are proceeding nicely." Grandfather tossed his glasses onto the stack of papers on the desk.

"You needn't look so smug." Jonathan walked to the windows and looked down on the storm-thrashed waves of Lake Superior. An early November squall lashed the windows with sleet, pinging off the glass and coating everything with ice.

"I can't tell you how happy I am you've signed those papers. I'm surprised you actually proposed to the girl, as unnecessary as that was, and bought her a ring. I suppose women like that sort of thing." He shrugged his thin shoulders. "The important thing is that the wedding will take place soon, before Christmas."

Jonathan clasped his hands behind his back under his suit coat and turned from the window. "I'm glad I could please you." The manipulating old goat. It galled Jonathan that he now actually wanted to do what Grandfather had been cramming down his throat for weeks. He'd have to put up with the gloating.

"I tell you, I was worried the whole thing would fall apart. I thought maybe you didn't want Kennebrae Shipping bad enough to go through with it. You've enough of me in you to have told me to keep it all and gone off to do your own thing. Don't think I haven't heard about the offers from other shipping companies to steal you away from me."

Jonathan walked over to the desk and leaned on his palms in front of Grandfather. "I know you think I'm merely obeying your orders, but understand this: I'm marrying Melissa Brooke because I happen to have fallen in love with her, not because it means I stay with Kennebrae Shipping. Melissa is intelligent, courageous, caring, and sweet. She's unspoiled, unselfish, and everything I want in a wife. Kennebrae Shipping has nothing to do with my marriage."

Grandfather leaned forward and thumped the desk. "Your marriage has everything to do with Kennebrae Shipping, and it's high time you knew it. Why do you think I chose Lawrence Brooke's daughter for you? He's settling a huge sum on you and his daughter at her wedding, and by sugar, we need it." He sat back, his breath rasping in his throat, his eyes gleaming.

A sick feeling of dread crowded into Jonathan's chest. "What do you mean, we need it?"

"I mean we're overextended. I've kept it from you boys, hoping I could turn things around, but it hasn't worked. I took an awful beating in the Depression of '93. I sank most of my capital into silver mining in Colorado. Then the market crashed. I carried on as best I could but gave myself apoplexy in the process."

He tugged at the blanket on his legs and refused to meet Jonathan's eyes. "Kennebraes are tough though. I weathered the storm. Things turned around, and as a gift to your grandmother, I built her Kennebrae House. She never knew how much I borrowed to build this place nor how much I borrowed to stay afloat during the recession. The only investment that has paid is Kennebrae Shipping."

Grandfather rubbed his hand along his jaw. "I can't draw any more capital from the shipping company. The shipping line needs capital to run, too. New boats, wages, fuel. We need Melissa's dowry to keep the fleet on the Great Lakes. We could lose it all without that money."

Jonathan straightened, numb, his mind frozen. "Why not just sell the other investments at a loss and get out? Keep Kennebrae Shipping viable. It's making money. I know it is. We're busier than we've ever been. You ordered four new ships."

Grandfather shook his head, his hands trembling. "Those four ships have yet to be paid for. And Kennebrae Shipping is security on the other investments. If those go down, so does the shipping line."

Jonathan swayed, reeling from this knowledge. Anger, shock, and disbelief crashed over him like the waves of the storm outside. Cold crept in from his limbs clear to his core. He turned back to the windows, unable to marshal his thoughts.

Kennebrae Shipping hung by a thread, the linchpin keeping all other aspects of the Kennebrae Empire from sinking without a trace. How had he not known? Was this partly his fault? He hadn't inquired into any of Grandfather's other dealings, concentrating only on the one business that fascinated him: shipping. And he'd concentrated on the day-to-day operations—contracts, scheduling, personnel. Grandfather had handled the financials, he and Wasserman. Jonathan had assumed it was in capable hands.

He swallowed hard, dread sinking like an anchor in his stomach. "You've duped us all. Me, Melissa, Lawrence Brooke, Almina. Even Noah and Eli. None of this has been for us—or even for Kennebrae Shipping. It's all been for you. So you don't have to look the fool for extending yourself too far. So you can keep up all this." He waved a hand at the opulent office. "This facade of wealth and power you've created. You haven't built an empire. You've built a house of cards."

Jonathan's anger grew with each word, building and cresting like a wave. "I'm ashamed. For the first time in my life, I'm ashamed to be a Kennebrae. What were you thinking, to use us all this way? It was bad enough when I thought you were just trying to manipulate me into marriage so you could get a new shipping contract. But to learn you've wagered all our futures on this stunt, I can't stand to even look at you. If I had known all this when you first raised the subject of marriage, I'd have told you to go jump in the lake. I'd have walked away from Kennebrae Shipping without a backward glance."

Grandfather challenged him with a glare. "You had that chance, and you didn't take it. You'd do anything for

Kennebrae Shipping. Because you were born to it. Because you know if you don't, you'll regret it. And all those workers, your captains, your crews you've spent so much time assembling, the dockworkers, all of them out of work with the stroke of a pen if you break the marriage contract. And don't forget the pensioners you've been carrying, those who've retired from Kennebrae. They'll be destitute if we go under. Be grateful you actually like the girl, get married, and solve all our problems."

"Are you really so arrogant, so full of yourself, sitting up here in your office dictating the lives of people like you're playing some game? The livelihoods of Kennebrae employees rest more on you than on me. I didn't sign away their security trying to build an empire. You did." He shook with anger, every muscle tense. "How could you be so foolish? I've a mind to walk out and let you pump your own bilges. Noah and Eli deserve to know about this. Did you plan their marriages to shore up some other falling bit of your sand castle? Have you thought for one minute what Grandmother would think of what you've done?"

This direst of questions hit the mark. Grandfather seemed to shrink before his eyes, becoming more frail and brittle. For long moments the only sounds in the room were his rasping breath and the crackle of the fire. "What are you going to do?" His voice came out weak, more subdued than Jonathan had ever heard it.

"I don't know, but I'll tell you this. Melissa must never find out. She'd be as humiliated as I. At least I can protect her from that. I wish I'd never signed your contract. You've effectively sold me and bought her. I hope you're happy." Jonathan stalked from the room, slamming the door behind him.

❧

Melissa sat at the piano, the rhythm of the Strauss piece flowing through her. Her fingers danced over the keys, bringing the music to life, her engagement ring winking back at her as she played. She loved waltzes. Her mind floated on the melody, her foot keeping the three-four time.

Her lips lifted in a smile. Soon she would waltz with Jonathan. The Shipbuilders' Ball on Thanksgiving night, the highpoint of the social calendar and only a week away. What would it be like to be held in his arms, skimming across the floor to the strains of a violin?

And Zylphia said there was a quadrille planned, too. Melissa hadn't been issued an invitation to dance the quadrille, for this one was only for those men and women who were single. Her engagement disqualified her from that particular event of the evening. No matter. She'd be attending the dance with Jonathan and could dance as often with him as she wanted. No frowning dowagers on the sidelines counting dances and gossiping.

The music trailed away as her fingers stilled. Mother and the modiste had designed a gown just for the occasion. Though Melissa had wanted to wear the gown she'd worn for the piano performance the night she met Jonathan, Mother's scandalized expression stilled her protests. No lady of high society appeared in the same dress twice. A social faux pas Melissa intended to commit as often as she pleased after her marriage. The expense and vanity of a new gown every night was ridiculous. If she liked something, she would wear it when it suited her.

The door opened, jarring Melissa from her reverie. "More flowers?" She turned on the piano stool. Sunlight streamed in the windows, washing the music room in a yellow glow, so much more cheerful than the steely gray skies and rain of the past few days.

"Yes, miss. Just arrived." Sarah's voice drifted through the mass of roses. She set the vase on the sideboard and brought Melissa the card. "Three bouquets this week. And perhaps another evening out?"

Melissa grinned at her maid and slit the envelope.

> *Dearest Melissa,*
> *Please accept my invitation to dine at the country*

*club this evening, and don't forget, it's opening night at
the Lyceum.*

*Affectionately,
Jonathan*

Since his proposal two weeks ago, Jonathan had courted
her, sending flowers, invitations, small gifts. Each came with
a card in his own hand. She'd saved them all in her jewelry
case. Every time they were together, she fell deeper in love.
He was interesting, intelligent, serious about business and
spiritual matters but able to laugh at himself. She twisted her
engagement ring, shaking her head. How silly that she'd ever
been opposed to this wedding. Now she counted down the
days like a child before Christmas.

She walked over to the vase and leaned to bury her nose
in the deep pink blossoms. The heady and familiar scent
enveloped her. Every time it was roses. Another wonderful
thing about Jonathan. He listened. Once, in passing, she'd
mentioned that roses were her favorite flower, and he'd
remembered. Hothouse roses this time of year would be so
costly, and yet he sent them often.

She checked the invitation again. Opening night at the
Lyceum. She smiled and stood the card at the base of the
flower arrangement where her mother would be sure to
see it. Mother would never guess the real meaning behind
the words.

"Sarah, come help me do my hair. I'm going out tonight."

fifteen

Jonathan smiled when she came into the Castlebrooke parlor. She wore his roses in her hair. They matched her pink gown perfectly. He quelled the stab of apprehension at not being forthright with her. It was for her own good that he didn't explain the Kennebrae finances.

Lawrence Brooke tucked his fingers into his vest pocket and looked her over, pride and satisfaction showing in every inch of his expression. "Ah, here you are. Very pretty."

Almina smiled indulgently. "Have a good evening. Your father and I will be out very late. We're dining at the Terrys'."

Lawrence frowned. "I don't know why you accepted their invitation, Almina. You know I don't like Roberta Terry. She's forever shoving women's suffrage down my throat. One of these times I'm going to forget myself and tell that woman just what she can do with her cause."

Jonathan's stomach muscles tightened. No wonder Melissa worried and sneaked out at night.

"Now, Lawrence, there's no harm in engaging in a discussion of the issue, and you enjoy Leonard's company. You'll have a good time."

He grumbled, checking his pocket watch. "Leonard would be wise to curb his wife's political passions. You won't see my wife touting such nonsense as women voting."

Jonathan winced at this all-too-prevalent viewpoint. He glanced at Melissa in the doorway. Her hands fisted at her sides, her chin lifted. Time to intervene.

He raised her hand, uncurling her tight fingers and placing a kiss on her fingertips. "You look stunning. I'll be the envy of every man tonight." He helped her with her cloak. "It's very cold. Will you be warm enough?"

Her jaw loosened. "I'll survive. And thank you for the flowers. I think we should be going, don't you?"

They took their leave of her parents, and Jonathan ushered her to his waiting carriage.

The maître d' showed them to an intimate table in a corner of the club dining room. Photographs and paintings of lake ships hung between high windows draped in gold fabric. Above Melissa's head, an oil of the *Bethany* hung in a gilded frame.

Jonathan lowered his gaze, not wanting to think about Kennebrae Shipping or the marriage contract in any way tonight.

Someone clapped him on the shoulder. "Well, how are you, Jonathan? It's been a long time."

Jonathan turned. "Mr. Fox." He mustered a smile, though he hated the intrusion, particularly by this small, barrel-chested man. Fox, an apt name for such a sly, cunning predator. "You're looking well." He rose and offered his hand, surprised anew at the power the older man's grip possessed. "Melissa, this is Gervase Fox of Keystone Steel. And may I introduce you to my fiancée, Miss Melissa Brooke."

"Ah yes, read about that in the paper. Delighted to meet you, my dear. It's about time someone caught this fellow and married him." Gervase beamed at Melissa then turned to Jonathan, his brow wrinkled. "Awful storms this past week. Did you suffer any damage?" He looked eager, rubbing his hands together, rocking on his toes. He licked his lips as if anticipating a juicy tidbit. Fox was the perfect name for Gervase. Even his whiskers grew up his cheeks like a fox's mask. And he didn't miss a trick.

Jonathan took delight in squashing his hopes. "No, sir, nothing important. As it happens, several of our ships were in port, here and in Two Harbors and Detroit. Only three were on the lake when the storms hit, and they were able to ride out the worst of it. A few minor repairs but nothing serious."

Gervase's mustache flattened in disappointment. "Good,

good to hear it. Some weren't so lucky. Wouldn't be surprised if the season ended early. I can feel it in the air, you know? And how's your brother, Noah? I've heard great things about him, hope to meet him while I'm in Duluth. Born to be a lake captain, that fellow."

"Noah's fine. Eager to get back out on the Lakes. The *Bethany*'s laid up for repairs at the moment. He's hoping for one last run of the season just after Thanksgiving." Manners forced Jonathan to ask, though he prayed the answer was no. "Would you care to join us for dinner?"

"Ah, you're kind to ask, son, but I'm dining with colleagues across the room. Just wanted to stop by and give you my best wishes. Congratulations on your engagement, young man. Looks like you've done well for yourself." He waved and departed, a small ship creating a big wake.

Jonathan relaxed his chest and arms, surprised at how tense he was. The state of the Kennebrae family fortune sat like a ton of iron ore in his chest.

"You look tired. Are you sure you want to go tonight?" Melissa reached across the table to grasp his hand where it lay on the white linen. "I can always go alone."

He squeezed her fingers. "I wouldn't dream of it. I am a little weary. Business is. . .tricky these days. But it will right itself soon."

She released his hand when the waiter brought their meals. The food was good, but Melissa only picked at hers.

"Something wrong?"

She shook her head. "It's just my father. You heard him tonight. If he knew what I was up to, his boiler would explode. He'd lock me in my room and put a guard at the door."

"I didn't realize he was so opposed to the idea of women voting."

"A lot of men are. I'm surprised you aren't, to tell the truth."

"Before I got a bang on the head"—he touched his temple lightly, smiling ruefully—"I hadn't given the idea much thought. Now that I've had time to consider it, I don't see the harm in it. In fact, I can see that it would be the right thing to do. Women have to pay taxes, have their sons and husbands conscripted into military service from time to time, have to obey the same laws and ordinances as men. I don't see why they shouldn't have a voice in the government that rules them."

"You've been reading our literature." She gave him a saucy grin, a pleased light in her eyes that quickened his heartbeat. "We'll make a suffrager out of you before you know what's what."

"If it means spending more time with you, I'm game." He sounded like a besotted fool, but he didn't care.

After dinner he helped her into his carriage, his breath hanging in a cloud of frost. He settled in beside her, contentment wrapping around him, only a tiny, niggling sense of unease marring the night. He searched for her hand, closing his around it.

She sighed. A comfortable silence enveloped them.

They headed west on Superior Street. The clopping of the horses' hooves on the pavement and the clatter of the carriage wheels drowned out the sound of the waves on the shore two blocks to the east.

Between the buildings he caught sight of the lighthouse guarding the piers that signaled the entrance to Duluth Harbor. The stark, skeletal frame of the new gondola bridge rose high above the water.

Ahead on the right, the Lyceum towered over the street, yellow light streaming from doors and windows. Carriages stood in a queue in front, disgorging passengers in furs and feathers for the opening night of the opera season.

"Are you sorry not to be going in?" He caught her profile in the lights as the carriage rolled by.

"No." He could hear the smile in her voice. "I don't really care for opera. Now if it was the symphony. . ."

The horses turned left onto Lake Avenue, toward the bridge and away from the Lyceum.

Kennebrae Shipping stood dark and imposing. He could make out the barest cracks of light around the third-floor corner windows. "Looks like someone's here already. They've got the blinds drawn." He swung the carriage door open and jumped down.

Their shoes crunched on the damp stairs.

The door opened a crack. A pale face studied them up and down then pulled the door wider. "Evening, sir. Didn't realize you'd be coming in tonight."

"Good evening, Dawkins. Any trouble?"

"No, sir. Them ladies is upstairs. No one else's been nosing around. I'm about to do another walk around the building now."

"Good. We'll go up ourselves. Carry on." Jonathan took Melissa's arm and headed toward the stairs, bypassing Grandfather's elevator. Their steps echoed on the marble treads.

"It's kind of spooky in the moonlight, but I bet it's beautiful in the day." Melissa craned her neck, looking up the staircase at the chandelier.

"It is. Grandfather never does anything by halves. The same architectural firm who designed Kennebrae House designed the offices, too. You'll have to stop by when the sun's shining. I'll give you a tour."

They stopped before an oak door with a frosted glass panel. The dim light from within silhouetted his name on the glass. He turned the ornate brass knob and held the door for her.

A single gaslight burned low on the far wall. Shadows draped the corners and furnishings. Their footsteps were muffled by a heavy, wool carpet. The familiar smells of paper, books, and ink wrapped around him. He breathed deeply. How he loved this place.

He led Melissa to the door beside the light. When he opened it, several ladies looked up from their work. He blinked in the sudden brightness but smiled at them. "Good evening, ladies."

"Oh, Mr. Kennebrae, thank you so much for letting us use your office. It's almost too nice to work in." One of the ladies, her hair straggling from a bun at her nape, bustled forward and all but bobbed a curtsy. She wrung his hand. "Come see what we've done."

He cast a glance over his shoulder at Melissa, who smiled at him, an imp of laughter in her eye. She loosened her cloak, revealing the pink evening gown. "Go ahead. I'll be fine."

"Mr. Kennebrae, you remember me? I'm Mrs. Britten. Beatrice Britten. We're so grateful for you helping us this way. Things are coming along so nicely for the rally. The sashes are done, see?" She pointed to the coatrack that had stood in the corner of his office only yesterday. Every peg bore dozens of purple, gold, and white sashes emblazoned with VOTES FOR WOMEN.

He admired their handiwork, glancing frequently at Melissa, who seated herself at a corner table with the English students. Fancy gown notwithstanding, he marveled at how she fit in with these ladies, most of whom wouldn't be received or even acknowledged by Almina Brooke and women of her social standing.

"And these are the banners." Mrs. Britten urged him to the conference table, awash with fabric, sewing baskets, and trim. She held up a white length of cloth. Someone had painstakingly stitched fabric letters in purple to spell out No TAXATION WITHOUT REPRESENTATION. Gold-fringe trim swayed and caught the light.

He read snippets of other slogans among the piles. END OPPRESSION OF WOMEN, WOMEN IN BONDAGE, FREE YOUR WIVES AND MOTHERS.

"We'll be finished with these in the next week or so. Then we'll go to making the badges and ribbons. The banners won't go on the poles until we get to the rally. It's so much easier to store them folded up."

Jonathan smiled ruefully. One of the many bookcases lining the walls of his conference room had been cleared, the books piled on their sides in columns on the floor. In their place, neatly folded, lay stacks of banners, looking like the Kennebrae House linen closet. When he'd said they could make themselves at home, they'd taken him at his word.

The ladies around the table followed his progress, expressions reserved though friendly. Their scrutiny made his collar tighten, though he couldn't blame them for having reservations. In their estimation he was a member of the enemy forces.

"I've heard nothing of the rally about town. Where is it to be held? In one of the parks? Are you marching down Superior Street?"

Mrs. Britten frowned. "We're not marching in Duluth until spring. These will be used first for the march on the state capitol in January. We'll be holding the rally in St. Paul on the opening day of the new session of Congress."

His gaze flew to Melissa. St. Paul? In January? "Melissa, could I see you for a moment?"

"I'll be right back, Synove." She nodded to her pupil. "You're doing well." Her skirt rustled as she rounded the long oval table. She bit her thumbnail.

Mrs. Britten turned to the table and busied herself moving fabric that didn't need to be moved.

Jonathan could almost see Mrs. Britten's ears twitching. "Were you planning on attending this rally in St. Paul?" He kept his voice low.

"Of course. I'm on the committee. I have to be there."

"And when were you going to tell me about it?"

"I hadn't given it any thought. I wasn't keeping it from you on purpose. I didn't think you'd be interested."

"We'll be married by then. Don't you think I would've noticed if you'd left town for a few days? How were you planning to get there, and who is going with you? You can't go alone. I don't know if I'll have time to accompany you."

She stiffened. "We're going by train. There are about fifty ladies going, and even if there weren't, I would be fine going by myself. I'm not a child, you know."

"Fifty women?"

She smiled. "Yes. The number was much lower a couple weeks ago, but thanks to Mother and the marriage contract, I now have the funds to charter two railcars to take us to St. Paul. She did insist I have my own money to use however I like once we're married."

Mrs. Britten turned around and frowned, shaking her head. "Don't say something like that, lass. He'll get the idea you're marrying him for money."

A cold sweat of guilt pricked Jonathan's upper chest and back. Marrying for money. He dropped his questions. The further he steered from that rocky shoal, the better.

sixteen

The distinctive clang of a hammer on metal reverberated through the boiler room of the *Bethany*. Jonathan ducked to enter the cramped space on the heels of Noah. Coal dust, oil, rust, and machinery smells assaulted him. He hunched his shoulders inside his wool coat. In dock as she was, the boilers were silent and cold.

"I wanted to inspect the progress myself!" Noah shouted above the noise. "I think we're a little ahead of schedule. Might be able to pull out on time after all. Day after Thanksgiving with a full load of ore."

Jonathan nodded. "That's only two days away. At least you'll be here for the Shipbuilders' Ball." His boots crunched on the iron grating of the gangway. The massive ribs of the ship curved along the walls, necessitating a careful watch lest he bang his head.

"They're double-checking the plating on the port side. We scraped the side of the lock up at the Soo on the last trip through." Noah shook his head, pursing his lips. "Should've taken the wheel myself. Let my first mate take us out."

"You treat this ship like your baby. If you could bring her home at night and tuck her into bed, you'd be happy."

"The only girl I'll ever love." Noah rubbed his gloved hand along the bulkhead, a grin splitting his bearded face.

"Captain?" A head appeared at the top of the steep stairs. "Someone on the dock asking permission to come aboard to see you."

Noah frowned. "Did he say who he was?"

"Said his name was Gervase Fox."

Noah raised an eyebrow at Jonathan. "I've heard of him. What's he want?"

"Don't ask me." Jonathan shrugged. "I knew he was in town, saw him at dinner one night."

Noah turned to the deckhand. "Send him to the wheelhouse. We'll meet him there."

They climbed the ladderlike steps from the belly of the ship to the spar deck then another flight to the cabin deck. The aft-most hatch lay open, giving them a long view down to the bottom of the hold. Noah tromped up another flight of stairs to the pilothouse, Jonathan on his heels. Everything about the day was raw, and being surrounded by so much frozen metal only drove the cold deeper into his bones. Jonathan didn't envy Noah a late November crossing. They had only a few minutes of stomping their feet and blowing on their hands in the tiny chart room behind the wheelhouse before the door opened.

Their visitor, rosy-cheeked and puffing, had to step rather high over the doorsill due to his small stature. "Colder than a spurned woman's heart out there." Gervase Fox stuck out his hand. "Good to see you again, Jonathan. I tried to call your office, but the operator said you aren't on the telephone line yet. When I stopped by your offices, they said you were down here. Why you'd be crawling about a hunk of steel in the harbor instead of inside by a warm fire, I'll never understand." The force of the little man's personality filled every inch of the chart room.

Jonathan shook his hand, not wincing as Gervase tried to crush his hand. "Always best to see for yourself where your money's going, don't you think? I'm sorry you had such a difficult time tracking me down. Grandfather's resisting installing a telephone, but he'll come around. Gervase, this is my brother Noah, captain of this vessel. Noah, this is Gervase Fox of Keystone Steel and Shipping."

Gervase's mustache bristled. "Captain. Pleased to meet you. I've heard good things about you. A hard-water captain who knows his ship and fears nothing."

Noah let the man pump his hand vigorously, while sending

an inquiring look to Jonathan.

Jonathan shrugged. "I hadn't realized you'd still be in Duluth, Gervase."

Gervase's eyes never stopped their piercing journey around the room. Just like a thief sizing up his next job. He'd have some reason for coming to Duluth, for hunting them down at the wharf, but Jonathan didn't expect him to reveal it too soon. "Ah, there's always business to conduct. And as you said, best to view where your money's going yourself. I'm looking into a few ventures. What do you know about Three Rivers Mining?"

Jonathan crossed his arms and leaned against the chart table. "Nothing to speak of. They have a mine near Biwabik. We might have carried some of their ore through a broker before. Couldn't say for certain though. You thinking of branching out into the ore mines?"

"Oh, it's worth a look while I'm in the area. I'll be up on the Mesabi Range at the end of the week, just nosing around, you know? I have a little capital to invest. How's your grandfather? I haven't seen him since he had the apoplexy."

Jonathan shifted his cold feet. "Grandfather's fine." He had better things to do than parry thrusts from this snake oil salesman. Why didn't he get to the point?

Gervase clasped his hands behind his back and bounced on the balls of his feet. "I heard tell he was trying to sell a brickworks in Erie. That so?"

Jonathan shrugged, trying to appear casual. "Possibly. He buys and sells all the time."

"Doing more selling than buying these days, I heard." Gervase shot him an intent look.

"Nothing wrong with consolidating, is there?"

Noah's brows came down at Jonathan's offhand tone.

Gervase put on a bland expression. "No, not at all, laddie." Then he grinned. "What say we shed this boardroom politicking and be straight with each other?"

"All right." Jonathan nodded but didn't let his guard down for a minute.

"I've heard rumors that Kennebrae is in trouble. A couple of his business partners have gone under, leaving him holding the bag on some sizable loans. But he's sitting on one golden egg of an asset." He swept his arm toward the bow. "Kennebrae Shipping. The largest fleet on the Lakes, four new boats set to slide off the shipyard ways this spring, and now a contract through marriage to transport most all the grain grown in the upper Midwest."

Jonathan swallowed and took a deep breath. "Not that I'm substantiating those rumors, but I have to wonder what concern it is of yours." *And how many other vultures are circling?*

Gervase looked him straight in the eye, all blandness wiped from his face, his eyes hard and glittering like Grandfather's when he struck a particularly lucrative and satisfying deal. "I might be in the market to buy Kennebrae Shipping. A sale now, when the share prices are so high, would net more than a tidy profit for Abraham and bail him out of some rather unpleasant troubles back East. His bankers are getting antsy."

The sheer boldness, the audacity of the man to come aboard this ship and make his bald offer took Jonathan's breath away.

"Now"—Gervase put up his hands—"I can see I've startled you, but there's no point in beating about the bush. Don't think I intend to turn you out of a job. I would want you—and your brothers—to stay on with the company. You've done well growing your business and your reputation over the past eight years. I've been watching. Kennebrae ships would be added to the Keystone Steel fleet, and you would head up the offices and operations here in Duluth. Nothing would change there."

Noah bombarded Jonathan with silent questions over Gervase's head.

Jonathan pushed them aside with a "later" gesture of his hand. "That's very kind of you, Gervase, but we're not looking to sell. Whatever rumors you've heard are false."

Gervase pursed his lips then clapped Jonathan on the shoulder. "Well, if you ever change your mind, let me know. I've got a job for you, either here or in Erie, if you ever want it. And I'll pay top dollar for Kennebrae Shipping when you're ready to sell." He wrung Jonathan's hand once more, waved a salute to Noah, and charged out the doorway. His footsteps on the metal ladder clattered through the framework of the pilothouse.

Noah crossed his arms and braced his feet apart. "What was that all about? Is Kennebrae Shipping in trouble?"

Jonathan's gut twisted. "Noah, we need to talk, but not here. Let's go to the office and warm up."

&

Back in the familiar comfort of his office, a roaring blaze in the fireplace, a mug of hot coffee cupped in his palms, Jonathan stretched his long legs and met Noah's intent, questioning stare.

Noah blew across his own cup. "Spill it. It's eating you alive, whatever it is."

Jonathan lay his head back against the burgundy wingback. "I'm sick about it. Grandfather's been wheeling and dealing, robbing one business to cover the losses of another. He told me about it two weeks ago, though he failed to mention the part about business partners doing a bunk and leaving him in the lurch. Apparently the whole empire—mines, mills, railroads—everything is hanging by a thread. The only thing holding it together is Kennebrae Shipping. The loans are due the first of the year, his credit's extended as far as it can go, and Kennebrae Shipping is the security for the loan."

Noah bolted to his feet, arms rigid, face frozen.

Jonathan knew just how he felt. Two weeks ago, he'd felt the same way. Two weeks of constant worry had worn off the edge.

"Why didn't you tell me?" Noah's hurt showed in his eyes. He paced before the fireplace.

Jonathan put down his cup and leaned forward, resting his forehead in his palms, elbows on knees. "I've done nothing but wrestle with the numbers and try to get a handle on just how far things have slid. I hoped he was exaggerating. I hoped it was just another of his Machiavellian maneuvers to ensure I'd marry Melissa. I'm sorry I didn't tell you as soon as I found out. I should have."

"How much money are we talking about?"

The sum drained the color from Noah's cheeks above his beard. He stopped pacing and gripped the back of his chair. He stared at Jonathan, his eyes burning hot bright blue like the center of a gaslight flame.

Jonathan understood. The *Bethany*, the *Jericho*, the *Nazareth*, two dozen other ships, Kennebrae House, all gone to satisfy the debt, and even then it might not be enough.

Realization spread over Noah's face. He took a steadying breath. "So we're going under?"

"No, we're not. Not if I have anything to do about it."

"All I can say, big brother, it sure is a good thing you're marrying money. Without Melissa's dowry, we'd be sunk."

Jonathan winced and picked up his cup. "Don't even breathe those words. If Melissa found out—"

He broke off as a gasp came through his office door. He sat bolt upright, spilling his coffee.

Melissa stood in the doorway, white as a Lake Superior fog, her hand gripping the doorknob. With a small cry, she whirled and ran down the hall.

seventeen

Melissa burst through the bronze and glass doors of Kennebrae Shipping and out onto the frosty street. The wind whipped her hair and clothes, slapping her cheeks with cold. The tears overflowed, tracking icy rivulets from lashes to chin.

Her coachman, Weatherby, stood at the heads of the team, his breath hanging in crystals. "Miss? Wasn't he there?"

She tried to speak, but no sound came out. She couldn't seem to draw a breath. Her heart hammered against her ribs.

"Miss?" Weatherby hurried to her side and grasped her elbow.

"I—I—can't breathe—can't breathe—" Her hand fluttered, and she gulped hard, trying to force air into her lungs.

"Easy, there." His gray eyebrows came down in a worried frown. He put an arm about her waist, edging her toward the carriage. "Just one slow breath." He sucked in a deep lungful, as if that would help her.

A short pant, and the air stuck in her throat again.

"No, nice and slow." His chest rose and fell once more.

This time more air got in.

"That's it. Are you all right? What happened?"

Before she could answer, the door banged open.

She whirled.

Jonathan Kennebrae, guilt written on every inch of his frame, stood in the doorway. "Melissa, wait."

She clung to Weatherby's hand. "Get me home, please. I don't want to talk to him."

The old man's eyes clouded with questions, but he obeyed, hustling her to the carriage and handing her inside.

Jonathan hurried down the steps toward her. His hand reached for the carriage door.

"Now, sir, you must be leaving the lady alone. She doesn't

want to see you right now." Weatherby interposed his frame between Jonathan and the open door. "I'll have to be asking you to step back."

"Don't be ridiculous. Melissa," he shouted over the coachman's shoulder, "if you'll just listen—" He broke off when Weatherby put his hand against Jonathan's chest and pushed him back.

Noah clattered down the stairs, blurry in Melissa's teary vision. "Jonathan, perhaps now isn't the best time." He grabbed Jonathan's elbow. "Or the place." With a nod he indicated the crowd of onlookers on the sidewalk.

Weatherby glared at both of them as he shut and fastened the carriage door. The carriage lurched and swayed. They were away.

Melissa dug in her bag for her handkerchief, pressing it to her mouth to stifle the sobs bursting from her throat.

She could only nod her thanks to Weatherby when he helped her out on the driveway at Castlebrooke. If only she could get inside without running into Mother.

The butler opened the door. "Good afternoon, miss. And how was your—" His voice broke off, eyes widening at her disheveled appearance.

She shook her head, tight-lipped, and hurried past, not bothering to take off her coat or hat. The route to her bedroom had never seemed so long before. She grabbed her skirts and ran up the stairs and down the hall to her sanctuary like a wounded animal heading to its den to nurse its wounds.

She slipped inside and leaned against the closed door. On wooden limbs she crossed the room and sank into her chair. Her hat tumbled to the floor, rocking gently on its crown. She shivered. The grate in the fireplace was cold since she'd expected to be out all afternoon.

In jerky movements she took off her gloves and unbuttoned her coat, feeling bludgeoned. Automatic motions took over as her mind whirled, refusing to settle on the one thing she must.

He lied.

It stabbed afresh, laying open her heart and dreams. Sobs

clogged her throat. She rose and flung herself onto the bed, crying uncontrollably, shoulders shaking, stomach clenching.

Everything. All of it. A lie.

Eventually the crying eased to a series of hiccups and sniffs. She flopped onto her back. A heavy band of tension settled around her forehead. She rubbed her gritty eyes. Every muscle ached, and every heartbeat throbbed with pain.

How could he do this to her? And how gullible was she to believe every word he'd said? What a brilliant plan, to pretend at first to be opposed to the marriage, affronted at the idea of being bartered away by their elders. Then, when she'd come to admire him, pretending he'd fallen in love with her. The flowers, the invitations, allowing the use of his office, the ring. . .

The ring.

She scowled down at the icy blue and white gems. With a sharp tug she yanked it from her finger, scratching her skin in the process. What should she do with it? She'd like to fling it back in his face. Her lips tightened.

The cad.

The satin duvet whispered when she rolled to the edge of the bed and sat up. She weighed the ring in her palm for a moment then whipped the token of his love and affection toward the fireplace. It clacked off the mantel and clattered to the hearth.

Lord, how could You do this to me? You promised me hope and a future. Plans that were for my good. He lied to me. All Your plans are dashed. It's over. Did You lie to me, too?

A tap at the door.

"Go away."

"Miss, there's someone to see you. Mr. Jonathan Kennebrae has called." Sarah.

"I don't want to see him. Tell him to go away."

"Miss, he's most insistent."

I'll just bet he is. The charlatan.

"I'm not coming down. He can wait until he's an old man for all I care." Melissa thumped the pillows with her fists and buried her face against them. Tears burned her throat.

Footsteps dwindled down the hall. She lay perfectly still, listening, until at last the front door closed.

ॐ

Jonathan walked as though he dragged the *Bethany*'s anchor chain with every step. How did a man cope when his worst fears were realized?

Lord, how can this be Your plan? If You can direct rivers in their courses, why can't You give me a way out of this mess? Is this where I'm supposed to say, "The Lord gives, and the Lord takes away. Blessed be the name of the Lord?" I'm not feeling that way.

He shoved his hands into his pockets, the cold biting through his suit jacket and shirt. Why hadn't he put on a coat? A gust of frigid, damp air swirled around him, nipping and numbing his cheeks.

He'd been in too much of a hurry, that's why. Chasing Melissa, trying to get her to listen to him, grabbing the first cab he could find.

And that supercilious snob they called a butler. Glowering as if he'd like to toss Jonathan out into the street like some mendicant ruffian. And the glare from the maid on the stairs hadn't helped either.

Could this day get any worse?

A streak plummeted past his nose, quickly followed by another. In dismay he glanced up toward Skyline Drive to see clouds boiling. The heavens opened like a washerwoman throwing out the rinse water. Jonathan was soaked to the skin before he reached Kennebrae House.

ॐ

Melissa straightened from bathing her face with cool water and looked in the mirror at her blotchy cheeks and puffy eyes. She dabbed with a folded towel then returned to her adjoining boudoir.

The remains of tea lay scattered across the tray on the low table before the fire. A fire roared in the grate, chasing the chill from the room. Lamps blazed, the bed was turned down invitingly, and Sarah straightened the tray to return it to the kitchen.

"You didn't eat anything." Her brown eyes looked mournfully into Melissa's, her mouth drawn into a disapproving pout. "You didn't have lunch either. Aren't you hungry?"

Melissa picked up her hairbrush and dragged it through her rumpled brown tresses. She shook her head. "I don't want anything to eat. Is Mother home yet?"

As if in answer, the door was flung open. Mother glided into the room, her skirts swaying, her expression fierce.

"What's this nonsense I hear about you quarrelling with Jonathan?"

Melissa braced herself, set the brush on the dressing table, and lifted her chin. "The marriage is off."

"Fiddlesticks. What utter foolishness. I don't know what sort of slight you imagine he's done you, but I assure you, the wedding will take place as planned."

"Never." *I'll run away first.*

"Stop acting like a child, and wipe all notions of running away from your silly head."

Melissa gasped.

"Oh yes, I know what you're thinking. Your expression says it all. But I want you to listen to me and listen well. You will attend the Shipbuilders' Ball the day after tomorrow as Jonathan's fiancée, and you will do so with grace and dignity."

"But, Mother, have you any idea—"

"I don't care to know the particulars. It doesn't matter."

"It doesn't matter to you that he's marrying me for money? That he doesn't care a whit about me?"

Mother rolled her eyes heavenward, as if pleading for assistance from above. "Of course he is. What did you think, that he was marrying you for—love? Don't be ridiculous. Love is a fleeting, traitorous emotion that is beneath you. Now, pull yourself together. You have a duty to this family and to Jonathan to behave with some decorum. The wedding contract has been signed, and there's nothing you can do about it."

Melissa narrowed her eyes and bit her thumbnail.

We'll see about that.

eighteen

"She sent them back, sir. The envelope is unopened." McKay set the vase of roses on the table by the office door. "And the chocolates came back, too." He handed the package to Jonathan.

The confections hadn't fared as well as the envelope. The box looked decidedly as if someone had stomped on it. He pitched it into the trash can and ran his fingers through his hair. How was he supposed to make things right when she wouldn't even see him? His lone hope lay in the Shipbuilders' Ball and Almina's promise that Melissa would be there. "Thank you, McKay. That will be all."

"Dinner is served, sir."

Thanksgiving dinner at Kennebrae House was a bust. Anticipating spending it with Melissa, Jonathan had waited in vain for an invitation. Noah was dining with friends across the harbor in Superior and would be coming to the ball from there. That left Jonathan and Grandfather, who never ate much anymore, to stare at each other over the roasted bird and trimmings. Grandfather's scowl and baleful glares did nothing to improve Jonathan's digestion.

Jonathan quit the meal long before the dessert course, stalking up to his room to stare into the fire. "Lord, I don't know where this is headed. I don't know how You can pull this from despair to hope. I don't know which way to turn now. You say the king's heart is in Your hand, and You can turn it however You wish. I've been praying pretty much nonstop that You would change Melissa's heart and cause her to hear me out, but You haven't been able to manage it. I feel like I've lost my anchor here and I'm drifting in a storm."

The clock on the mantel chimed six. Time to dress. More

weary than he could remember, Jonathan pushed himself up from the chair. At least it wasn't a masquerade ball this time. Last year he'd borne with stoicism maidens in costume and men in turbans and pointy shoes, Russian hussars, and three different Napoleon Bonapartes. His own costume, ordered and insisted on by Grandfather, at least had a bit of dignity to it. He'd gone as Admiral Lord Nelson.

Would she come? Would she give him a chance to explain? And if she did, what could he say? Why should she believe him? He fumbled with his tie, fingers clumsy as his mind raced. And if he couldn't make her understand, if she broke the marriage contract, what would happen to Kennebrae Shipping?

He yanked the ends of his crooked bow tie and snatched up his hat. "McKay! Where are you? Come help me with this thing!"

Finally put together with the butler's help, he trotted downstairs.

Grandfather, resplendent in evening dress with a cunningly cut jacket made especially not to bunch or wrinkle in his wheelchair, waited by the door. A black satin lap robe covered his legs. Shiny black shoes rested on the foot tread.

Jonathan stopped short. "I didn't know you were coming."

"I'm going along to see you don't foul things up more than you already have." Grandfather pulled on his gloves and accepted his cloak and hat from McKay.

A direct hit. Grandfather had the ability to pierce Jonathan's reserve like no other. Except Melissa. In fact, his desire to shout at both of them bubbled and hissed like lava under pressure. He was a man nearing explosion. He rode in stony silence to the club.

The country club lights shone like diamonds, casting winking beams on the lake. Carriages and automobiles packed the long, curved drive, passengers arriving in a steady stream at the wide front doors. The night air held the tang of snow, and the breeze off the lake hit his skin like ice water.

Jonathan clenched and unclenched his hands on his thighs as they awaited their turn to go inside. He mentally rehearsed and discarded several opening lines.

The coachman opened the door and pulled out the custom-made ramp to accommodate Grandfather's chair.

A blast of warmth hit them in the foyer. Attendants led ladies upstairs to lay aside capes and coats and freshen their appearances, while the gentlemen swirled off cloaks and stuffed gloves into top hats, and placed them in capable hands in the coatroom. Music drifted down the hallway from the ballroom.

Jonathan wheeled Grandfather toward the sound. A waltz in progress greeted their eyes beyond the gilded doors. Pinwheels of color in the ladies' dresses, stark black stiffness in the men's attire, and overall the golden glow of six crystal chandeliers bolstered by countless wall sconces.

He saw many familiar faces, business colleagues, shipping rivals, church friends, but not the one he so desperately sought. The knot in his stomach tightened. Where was she?

"Stop looking like a condemned man and get me some punch." Grandfather poked him in the leg. "She'll be here."

❧

Melissa winced as the cold beads touched her throat.

Sarah fastened the five-string choker of perfectly matched pearls. From the center a sapphire and diamond pendant hung, reflecting the dressing table lights. "It's perfect, miss."

"Almost." Mother tapped an ivory folded fan against her palm. "Where's the ring?"

Melissa glanced down at her bare hand. "I'm not wearing it."

"Yes, you are. All of Duluth society will be there tonight, they've heard about the ring, and they'll want to see it. Where is it?" She stalked to the dresser and opened the jewel case.

"I don't know. I threw it away."

Mother whirled, mouth agape. "You what? You little fool!" She advanced on Melissa, cheeks red, eyes blazing. "You're ruining everything. Do you want me to be the laughingstock of all Duluth society?"

"Why won't you listen to me? Jonathan is only marrying me so he can get his hands on Father's money. If nothing else, this marriage isn't a sound investment for Father."

"You know nothing about such things. Let the men handle the business end. You'll do your part like a dutiful daughter and keep your nose out of business affairs. Your liberal notions are making you overstep your bounds. You won't mention a word of this to your father, and if you've lost that ring. . ."

Sarah stepped forward. "Ma'am, the ring's not lost." Her voice cracked. "It was on the hearth when I swept up this morning." She hurried to Melissa's jewel case on the dresser and withdrew the ring.

Mother snatched it from her hand and pushed her aside. "Put it on."

Melissa bowed her head, shoulders slack. She held out her hand for the ring. Would she ever have a say in her own future? Pawns and bartered chattel had no say at all.

"We'll be leaving in five minutes. Do not make me come up and get you." Mother stormed from the room, her heels clacking down the hall.

"I'm sorry, miss."

"It's all right, Sarah." Melissa slipped the ring on and looked in the mirror.

Melissa came down the stairs on the dot of her mother's deadline.

Mother looked her over from coif to slippers, taking note of the engagement ring with icy satisfaction. Father frowned, preoccupied as always, then helped Melissa with her cloak.

The atmosphere in the automobile was even colder than the air outside. No one said a word.

Lord, just help me get through tonight with some dignity. I will not marry a man I cannot trust.

Her mother took her by the arm and ushered her into the ladies' changing room, standing guard with crossed arms while Melissa hung up her cloak and checked her appearance.

Melissa stared into her own eyes, building her resolve. She lifted her chin. Dignity.

Thankfully one of Mother's friends drew her attention away from Melissa when they emerged into the hall, and Melissa was able to go downstairs alone.

Zylphia pounced on her at the bottom of the grand staircase, her mint green silk swishing. "Ooo, you look beautiful. What a perfect gown. Did the modiste make it?" She squeezed Melissa's arm. "Indigo velvet. Now why didn't I think of that? It makes your eyes so blue."

Melissa tried a smile. "Your dress looks just right. You'll have men lining up for dances."

"Actually, my card's already full." She held up a wrist from which dangled a tasseled ivory booklet. "I'm having the next waltz with"—she consulted her list—"Frank Strand." A satisfied smile played on her lips. "You're lucky to be engaged. You can dance with Jonathan all you want. Where is he, by the way?" She looked over the crowd. "You can hardly find anyone in this crush."

Melissa fervently hoped Zylphia was right. Nothing would suit her more than to avoid Jonathan all evening.

God did not see fit to grant her wishes. Jonathan approached through the milling guests, tall and lean and devastatingly handsome in evening dress.

She chided her traitorous heart for flipping like a landed fish in her breast.

"Good evening, ladies." He bowed from the waist. "You look lovely."

Zylphia giggled and held out her hand. "Thank you, Mr. Kennebrae."

"Please, call me Jonathan. I'm sure, as a friend of Melissa's, we shall see quite a lot of each other in the future." He smiled, but Melissa noted the strain around his eyes.

Stop it. He's feeling no pain. He knew all along it was a lie.

"Melissa"—he turned to her—"I'd like a word with you in private, if I may."

"No, you may not. Leave me alone."

Zylphia swung around to stare at Melissa. Her mouth dropped open. "Melissa?"

Jonathan set his jaw like granite.

The heat of wounded anger built in Melissa.

A voice broke into their conversation. "Ladies, Jonathan, we just got here. Wicked cold on the harbor tonight." Noah Kennebrae clapped Jonathan on the shoulder. "The music's starting, and if it isn't too brash, I'm going to steal a dance with my future sister-in-law. Come, Melissa, before he occupies all your time this evening."

Noah grabbed her hand and tugged her onto the dance floor.

Helpless to stop him without causing a scene, she went into his arms.

nineteen

Noah leaned to whisper in her ear. "Melissa, you have to give him a chance to explain. It isn't what you think."

She sent him a cold glance, stiff with indignation at being maneuvered into dancing with Jonathan's brother, forced to listen to him plead Jonathan's case. "It is exactly as I think. There's no mistake. Kennebrae Shipping is in trouble, and Jonathan cast about for a wealthy bride to bail him out. I don't blame him for that. It is hardly uncommon these days, though I think it is a calloused and mercenary approach to marriage."

"Then what are you blaming him for? Sending back flowers, returning gifts. Hardly the behavior of a proper fiancée." He quirked an eyebrow at her.

She swallowed hard, forcing back the ever-ready tears of late. She would not cry. "I blame him for lying to me. For pretending he felt some tenderness, that he cared for me as a person rather than a bank account. The man has a strongbox for a heart that he could perpetrate such a charade. It's cruel and unfeeling."

Noah frowned. "I think it is high time you learned a few things about my brother. Jonathan's guarded his heart and feelings for a long time, protecting them under plating thicker than the hull of my ship. But that isn't because his heart is cruel and unfeeling. It's because his heart feels too much, is too tender to trust to just anyone. I was mighty happy when I saw him falling in love with you. He was more content, more at peace than I'd ever seen him. I don't think he lied when he professed his feelings for you."

Melissa had been hurt too deeply to allow a few words to change her mind. "I know what I heard."

Noah gave her a little shake, pivoting her sharply. "You know what you think you heard. I'm the one who made the

126

clumsy remark. Not Jonathan. I'm the one you should be angry at. Stop taking my thoughtlessness out on my poor brother. He's heartsick to think you've been hurt. If you could've heard him rounding on me after you ran away from him in the street, you'd know how badly he's taking this."

She shook her head. "But is it true? Is Kennebrae Shipping in financial trouble? Will marrying me save the company?"

Noah's lips flattened, his brows coming down. "I won't lie to you, Melissa. Grandfather's in a precarious state, moneywise. There is no denying your dowry would patch his leaky boat. But that's irrelevant to what Jonathan feels for you. I'm telling you he loves you and would marry you if you came to him with nothing more than the clothes you stood up in. Just give him a chance. Talk to him. Let him explain."

The music ended. Melissa dropped her hand from his shoulder and applauded politely for the orchestra. Could she trust Noah when he stood to gain from her believing him? Was he playing her just like Jonathan?

"Please, Melissa, give him a chance." He led her to the sidelines.

Mother waited with Abraham Kennebrae. Her icy fingers dug into Melissa's arm. "There you are, dear." The words came out falsely bright between clenched teeth. "I've been looking all over for you."

"My fault, Mrs. Brooke. I snatched her up for a dance from under Jonathan's nose." Noah bowed to Melissa. "Thank you, Melissa, and think about what I said. You won't be sorry." He winked and turned on his heel.

Abraham took Melissa's hand between his dry palms. "You look lovely, my dear girl. A credit to us all."

Melissa mustered a smile, though she longed to yank her hand from his grasp. Here sat the originator of her misery, like a king holding court, and they all danced to the tune he called. It wasn't fair, not to her and not to Jonathan either.

And Mother was no better, standing at his shoulder like a vizier, carrying out his plans with relish. And to what purpose? If Mother believed her that the Kennebrae Empire teetered on the brink of financial disaster, that it was her husband's money that would shore it up, would she be so eager to push this marriage?

A hand touched her elbow. "May I have this dance?" Jonathan's voice was velvet smooth, but there was an iron look to his eye.

"Of course you may," Mother answered for Melissa. "Go, enjoy yourself. We'll be waiting right here for you." Her tone forbade argument.

Melissa, perforce, went into Jonathan's arms, stiff as a mannequin.

"If you don't relax and stop pushing away from me, you're going to topple over backwards," Jonathan spoke to the top of her head. "You weren't this rigid when you danced with Noah just now."

"Noah is a good dancer." She refused to look up at him, refused to acknowledge the bittersweet pain of her palm in his, his hand at her waist.

"Most sailors are. But my dancing prowess, or lack of it, isn't the reason you're acting like you want to bolt from my arms. Either you listen to me here on the dance floor and stop acting like you're heading to your own execution, or I'll toss you over my shoulder and carry you out of here like the brat you're being. And believe me, I won't care a whit for the scandal it causes."

She looked up into his stormy brown eyes. He'd do it, too. She relaxed a fraction and allowed him to draw her closer to match his steps.

"That's better. Melissa, I want to apologize for Noah. He spoke without thinking. But I can assure you, I never lied to you. I didn't even know about Grandfather's problems when I proposed to you. I signed those marriage contracts as a gesture of obedience and honor to your father and my grandfather. The money means nothing." He let go of her hand to lift her chin. "Melissa Brooke, I love you. I don't care about Kennebrae Shipping. I don't care about Brooke Grain. I care about you."

She looked into his eyes, the feelings brimming there, and steeled her waffling, traitorous heart. *Don't trust him. He's lying to you again.*

They came to a stop near the edge of the dance floor. Melissa's thoughts whirled.

He led her through the crowd toward where her mother and his grandfather sat. "I'd like nothing more than to get out of here, to go someplace we could talk. I have so much to say to you, so much to ask your forgiveness for. You don't know the half of it yet."

Abraham's papery old voice reached them in a lull in the noise. "Frankly I was surprised by your letting Melissa go to those suffrage movement meetings. And in the middle of the night, too. But you don't need to worry. Jonathan will put a stop to it as soon as they're wed."

Melissa's heart felt like the bottom had opened and the contents drained out. She glanced at her mother.

Almina's eyes flashed fire, her face blazing. Her mouth opened and closed like a screened door in the wind.

Jonathan's grip tightened on Melissa's arm.

She wrenched it away. A liar and a snitch. "You told your grandfather?"

Jonathan spread his hands in an appealing gesture. "Melissa, I promise you I didn't—"

She tugged at the ring on her finger. Jagged ice coated her insides. She pressed the ring into his hand. "Good-bye, Jonathan."

twenty

"Are you sure you want to do this?" Noah hoisted his duffel and stepped onto the gangplank. "I don't like it."

Jonathan nudged his brother ahead. "I'm sure. There's nothing keeping me here."

"You know you're welcome aboard, but I can't help feeling this is a mistake."

"Enough. I don't want to talk about it anymore."

Steam hissed gently, a steady *thrum* vibrated through the ship. The firemen must be stoking the boiler.

"Put your things in my cabin, and take my duffel, too." Noah handed Jonathan his bag. "I'll be aft checking with the engineer. We'll be underway in about half an hour."

Jonathan wove his way forward through deckhands grappling ropes, carrying provisions to the galley, and swarming over the pilothouse. Piles of slushy snow lay on the hatch covers, and ice rimed the rails. A week's snow squalls had kept a fleet of vessels in port, but the day, though cold, looked fair. Relief at their departure curled around the guilty despair in Jonathan's middle. If they could just get away.

He shouldered his way through the narrow door to Noah's cabin. Twice the size of the other accommodations aboard ship, it was still smaller than the china closet at Kennebrae House.

His brother's bag fit in the locker beside the door, but there was no room for Jonathan's possessions. He slung his valise under the desk. That would do for now. Three steps took him the length of the room. Frost prevented his looking out the portal. But the air in the cabin was warming up, steam whispering through pipes overhead heating the space.

Jonathan lay down on the bunk and clasped his hands behind his head. Footsteps on rungs, clanking pots from the galley down the hall, the ring of metal on metal, and under it all, the growl of the boilers.

Sick at heart. He'd heard the term before, but not until now did he realize the truth of it. He tried to relax, to allow the slap of water against the hull to ease his tension, but failed miserably.

He shifted, bringing his arms down and lacing his fingers over his middle. The crackle of paper made him frown. He dug in his coat pocket and withdrew several sheets of folded documents. His marriage contract. Lawrence Brooke had returned it to him three days ago, the morning after the Shipbuilders' Ball.

They'd stood in the foyer at Castlebrooke. Melissa refused to see him. Almina glowered at him, her look accusing him of ruining Melissa's reputation by revealing her suffrage activities and abetting her in conducting them under cover of darkness. He could shrug off Almina's accusations. But he couldn't shrug off Lawrence's words.

"I'm sorry, Jonathan. This isn't going to work. I've tried, Almina's tried, even Pastor Gardner tried. She's adamant. When we first put this thing together—your grandfather and I—I thought you two could come to an understanding, that Melissa would acquiesce to my wishes and you'd make a sound match. I had no idea she was entangled in this nonsense about women voting, and I wouldn't ask any man to marry her until she shed such foolishness. The fact that she remains so resistant to meeting with you shows me that the damage is irreparable. I can see now that your marriage would be a mistake. And as things stand between the families now, it would be better if we discontinued any business dealings as well." He'd thrust the papers into Jonathan's hands and walked away. "My lawyers will see to the dissolution of the contracts."

Jonathan's anger had kept him warm on the ride back to Kennebrae House. Without bothering to take off his coat, he took the stairs two at a time up to Grandfather's office.

The argument they had, the harsh words they'd hurled at

one another now echoed in his head, swirling, clashing, aching.

The door swung open. Noah came in, unfolding a cot. "I know there's not much room, but I figured you'd rather bunk in here with me than with the men. We've a full crew and no racks to spare. It's either this or a hammock strung in the crew mess." He wrestled with the canvas and wood, knocking it against the wall, the bunk, and the locker until he finally crashed it down into the corner. "There, and you can have my extra pillow."

"Thanks, Noah." Jonathan swung his feet over the side of the bed and sat up. He put his head in his hands. "We should be pulling out soon, right?"

Noah closed the door and pulled the desk chair out with his foot. "There's quite a wait, I'm afraid. And we just got word the *Capernum*'s laid up. We're going to tow her consort, the *Galilee*, along with us. It's loaded and ready to go. We'll pick her up from the Number Three Dock." He sank onto the chair and clomped his boots up onto the cot. "We have time for a little chat."

"Noah, we've been through this. I don't want to talk about it." Jonathan lifted his head long enough to frown at his brother.

"Well, I do, and we've got nothing better to do until they signal us for our turn to pull out. Did you say good-bye to Grandfather?"

"No. I haven't spoken to him since Friday. We've said all we need to say to one another."

"I can think of a few things you haven't said that need saying."

"Like what?"

"How about, 'I'm sorry?'"

Jonathan looked up. "Are you serious? After what he's done? He should be apologizing to me. Manipulating, conniving, double-dealing, then dropping the boom on everyone by blabbing about Melissa's suffrage work. Then having the nerve to tell me it was all my fault things fell apart like they did. He's blaming me!" He thumped his chest with his fist. "I told him he could keep it—Kennebrae Shipping, Kennebrae House, all of it. He made his bed; now he can just lie in it. I told him to contact Gervase Fox and unload what he could to keep his head above water. That's all I can do."

Noah stroked his beard, his eyes troubled. "And what of Melissa?"

Jonathan winced at her name. "It's over, and you know it. She gave the ring back. The contract's broken. She wouldn't see me."

"Funny, when all this started, you were dead set against the marriage, couldn't wait to find a way out of it. Then you went and fell in love with the girl. Not that I blame you. She's great. If you weren't so right for her, I'd have a go at trying to win her myself." He grinned.

"Good luck." Jonathan lay back on the bunk again. He pressed his palm to his heart, feeling the cold lump of a sapphire and diamond ring in his inner coat pocket.

Noah let his feet thud to the floor. "And you say Grandfather's stubborn. You love her, and I know she loves you, too. And here you are, set to sail out of the harbor, your tail tucked firmly between your legs, afraid to fight to get her back."

Jonathan said nothing, angry and weary of the topic altogether.

"Well? Are you going to fight for her?"

"The fight is over. I lost. Now leave me alone." He rolled to face the wall.

After long minutes the door clicked shut. Noah's footsteps echoed in the passageway.

❧

Melissa's shoulders sagged. The newspaper crackled as it fell to her lap. That article, bold as brass on the front page, blaring to the world about her broken engagement. And missing the truth by several leagues.

Sarah, her only companion of the past three days, knelt by the fireplace and swept the grate. The maid had managed to smuggle the paper up to Melissa.

Mother had tried to hide it from her, but Melissa wanted

to know the worst.

Melissa sighed, her chest heavy, and raised the paper again. "'November 24. Brooke-Kennebrae Wedding Sunk—The Shipbuilders' Ball of 1905 will long be remembered for its fireworks. No, not those shot off the end of the dock at midnight but those that took place in the ballroom between the Brooke and Kennebrae families. Melissa Brooke, daughter of Lawrence and Almina Brooke of Duluth, ended her engagement to Jonathan Kennebrae of Kennebrae Shipping publicly. Scuttlebutt says a difference of opinion regarding giving women the vote is at the root of this surprising turn of events. Our sources tell us Miss Brooke has been engaged in an underground suffrage movement in the Duluth area for some months. Mr. Kennebrae, left flat-footed and stunned on the dance floor, has our sympathies.'"

Tears stung Melissa's eyes, but she blinked hard and continued reading. "'For several weeks the Brooke-Kennebrae nuptials have taken a great portion of this column's ink: wedding gifts, guest lists, flowers, music, the intimate details provided us by Mrs. Almina Brooke. It seems such a waste, and the wedding of the year, set for just three weeks from tomorrow, is now officially off. Neither Miss Brooke nor Mr. Kennebrae could be reached for comment. Mr. Kennebrae's office has informed us of his imminent departure for Erie, Pa.' aboard the cargo steamer, *Bethany*, at the beginning of next week. Perhaps he made a lucky escape.'"

Sarah sat back on her heels, her mouth drawn down. "I'm sorry, miss. They have no cause to talk about you that way."

"It's all right, Sarah. They got so much wrong that it's like they're talking about someone else."

"I got your note down to Mrs. Britten. She said Peter and Wilson would deliver word to all the ladies not to come tonight. And she'd arrange with Kennebrae's to get all the things out of Mr. Kennebrae's office as soon as possible."

Melissa closed her eyes and rested her head against the back of the chair. "I'll have to get word to Mrs. Britten to cancel the chartered train. I won't have the money for it now."

Mother entered, her mouth pinched, eyes narrow. She sagged into the chair opposite Melissa.

Sarah averted her gaze and hurried from the room. Melissa wished she could do likewise.

"I've spent all day canceling wedding arrangements. The florists, the food, the orchestra. You have no idea."

"I'm sorry, Mother. I wish there was something I could do to help." Melissa said the words carefully, knowing the knife-edge her mother walked with her temper these days.

"You've helped enough. I see you've read that wretched article. I'll never be able to show my face at the club again, thanks to that awful reporter. And I might as well forget ever being invited to the bridge club or the garden society. I'm a pariah in this town."

"I know how difficult all this has been for you." Melissa couldn't keep the dryness from her tone. Mother's martyrdom had grown tiresome.

"How like you to be sarcastic. You've no care at all for the consequences of your actions. You never have. If you had thought how this would play out, you'd have bitten your tongue, kept your radical ideas to yourself, and gotten married as I wanted. Now I don't know what we'll do with you. You can't stay here. Perhaps it would be best if you were to take an extended trip out to your father's Aunt Persephone in San Francisco."

"Oh no, please. Her house is like a mausoleum, and she smells of vegetable tonic."

"I daresay she does. However, you have no further say in this mess of your making. You'll do as you're told for once."

Melissa sat staring at the closed door when Mother left. The ache in her heart, the yearning emptiness, threatened to swallow her whole. Alone, she could contemplate the last lines of the article. Jonathan was leaving—leaving her to face the town's curiosity alone, to take the blame that belonged to him. His betrayal was complete.

&

Jonathan finally levered himself off the bunk and headed to the wheelhouse. He braced himself against the roll of the ship, surprised at the strength of the waves. The clanging of the channel-marker buoys and harbor sounds slid behind them. The engine hummed, propelling them through the chop. He couldn't stay in the cabin for the entire journey. He'd go mad.

Up one flight then out onto the deck. He gripped the rail and looked over the side. The *Bethany* rode low in the water, her hold laden with iron ore, showing about twelve feet of freeboard. Waves curled back, creamy white over greenish gray along her hull.

Gulls cried and keened along the shore off the port side. He looked astern, past the consort barge, *Galilee*, to Duluth growing steadily smaller.

Kennebrae House's slate mansard roof jutted skyward, its solid frame dark against the hillside. Almost abeam of them, the gray walls of Castlebrooke rose, stately and smooth. She was in there, angry and hurt, stubborn and unwilling to listen to reason. Believing he had betrayed her and refusing to let him explain.

He turned from the rail, disgusted at himself. Up another flight to the chart room and through to the wheelhouse.

A sailor stood at the wheel, Noah behind him on a high chair. Jonathan noted his frown. "What is it?"

Noah tapped the barometer on the wall beside him. "The bottom's dropping out of this thing. Harbor forecast said cold and fair. But I don't like the look of this. The wind's picking up. I think we're in for some rough seas."

At that moment a patter of sleety rain hit the windows. A wave slapped the bows, scattering spray upward. The ship lurched but plowed on.

Jonathan shrugged. His life had been nothing but stormy seas of late. What was one more blow?

twenty-one

Conditions worsened rapidly. Fitful snow turned into squalls then a raging blizzard. The seas grew rougher, mounting before a gusting wind.

"Keep us pointed into those waves," Noah ordered the helmsman. "If we fall sideways into a trough, we might capsize." He ducked in front of the wheel and dialed the chadburn to ALL-AHEAD FULL. A bell rang below them, and the engine room answered back with "All-ahead full." The throb of the engine increased in pitch.

Noah spoke into a tube on the wall. "Put two more men down in the boiler room. Keep those fireboxes full. We're going to need every ounce of power to stay on course."

Jonathan anchored himself against the pitching of the ship by grabbing the door frame. A bell chimed, twice, a pause, then once.

"It's seven thirty in the second dogwatch." Noah kept his eyes forward. Snow scoured the windows. "The watch will change in half an hour."

"Captain, I see the Two Harbors light."

Jonathan peered over his brother's shoulder through the growing gloom, waiting. "I don't see it."

"Wait for it, sir."

Ahead and to port, a faint, lighter spot in the haze then darkness.

A mighty wave burst over the bow, raining ice water over the pilothouse. The engine surged as the wave rippled down the vessel and lifted the propeller clear of the water for a moment.

Jonathan noted the helmsman's white face, knuckles gripping the wheel, straining to see through the dark.

Noah didn't look much better, though his voice remained

calm. "Right rudder ten degrees." He consulted the compass. "Stay clear of the shoals."

"Should we try to make Agate Bay, Captain?"

"No, I don't think we could make the harbor in these conditions. I don't fancy plowing into her seawall in the dark."

For long hours they forged ahead through the worsening storm. Jonathan went between the galley and the wheelhouse, bringing coffee and food to his brother who refused to rest. The temperature plummeted into the teens then into single digits. Ice formed on the rails and decks, making maneuvering about the boat difficult and dangerous.

A seaman, drenched and dripping, ducked into the tiny room. "Captain, the waves are breaking over the spar deck."

"Are the hatches holding?" Noah staggered as the *Bethany* slewed. He grabbed the window ledge to steady himself. "Are we taking on water?"

"The bilge pumps are coping, sir, but just barely."

"Very well. Any word from the *Galilee*?"

"None, Captain. But it's rough out there. The line's staying taut."

"Go back and watch that line. I wish we'd doubled the hawsers in harbor."

The seaman tugged his hat on tight and shouldered open the door.

"Can we make Isle Royale? Anchor in the lee of the island, sir?" The helmsman's voice rose with each question.

Jonathan's unease grew. "Noah—" A monstrous wave crashed against the ship, jerking her almost sideways. Jonathan was slung to the floor, striking his head against the captain's chair bolted to the floor. For a moment stars shot through in his vision. He righted himself, accepting his brother's hand to help him up.

Water sluiced down the windows, blinding the men with every wave. Winds buffeted the ship, pushing so hard that even with the engines at maximum capacity, she made no headway.

"Captain, we're listing to starboard. The pumps are falling behind, sir."

"That's it." Grim lines of worry etched Noah's face. "We've got to turn around and make for Duluth."

The call for all hands rang through the boat. The first mate, his face ashen, climbed into the already crowded wheelhouse. "Captain, are you sure?"

"Yes, Meroff. We've no choice. At the rate we're burning coal, we'll run out before we get halfway across the lake. Without power we'll be at the mercy of the waves."

"But those troughs! We'll roll for sure."

"Meroff!" Noah scowled at him. "Get to your station. Stand by to come about."

The man gave an abashed look, his eyes wide. "Aye, Captain."

Jonathan wiped his hand down his face. What Noah proposed was exceedingly dangerous. In order to come about, he'd be putting the *Bethany* broadside to the waves. If he couldn't swing her bow around quickly, they'd be caught in the trough and rolled over like a piece of driftwood. But with the ship listing and running short of coal, Jonathan knew his brother had no choice.

"Jonathan, would you pray?" Noah's blue eyes pierced Jonathan.

He nodded. "God, our Father, Master of the waves and the wind, we ask Your protection on this vessel and on the lives of these men." Jonathan spoke loudly over the screaming wind and pounding waves.

Noah shot him a grateful glance.

"We're humbled before the power of Your creation. But we know You hold us in the palm of Your hand. Nothing will happen to us that isn't in Your will. Give Noah clarity of mind and certainty of purpose. We thank You for bringing us this far. Please help us now. Amen."

Every man in the pilothouse echoed that Amen.

Jonathan didn't quit praying, and he knew Noah was praying, too.

"Right full rudder," Noah gave the order. "Hang on, men."

The bow swung around, blasted by water and wind. Snow scoured the windows, blocking their vision. Every man braced himself as the *Bethany* slid sideways and down. The descent seemed to last forever. Would they ever reach bottom?

Jonathan glanced out the porthole beside him. Only raging lake water was visible. Were they already rolling over?

"More steam!" Noah shouted into the talking tube.

The stern of the boat lifted clear of the water, the prop spinning wildly, shuddering through the vessel. A wave lifted them stern first, the nose plowing down.

Somewhere below a man screamed, "Father, save us!"

Jonathan's mouth dried to dust. His hands ached from gripping the door frame.

One of the front windows cracked, letting in a gust of frigid air and a fine spray of ice water. The enormous wave picked them up and slung them forward. The roar of the storm was immense, buffeting them.

The helmsman let out a cheer, grinning wildly at the captain. "We made it! You did it, sir!"

Noah didn't answer his grin. He skidded over to the ladder and shouted to the deck below, "Check on the *Galilee*! See if she made it around."

Jonathan ducked through the doorway into the chart room, peering through the water and blackness toward the stern. He could see no more than a few feet.

The ship shuddered and groaned but forged through the seas.

He returned to the wheelhouse. "I can't see a thing out there. Noah, are we going faster now?"

"The wind and waves are pushing us along now instead of us fighting through them." Noah turned to the chadburn and sent the message to dial back the engines. "We'll save some coal. It won't take as much to maintain steerage heading in this direction."

"Was that as close as I think it was?" Jonathan hunched into his coat, stepping back to get out of the draft from the cracked window.

"Closer. God sure was with us." Noah resumed his chair. "Thank you for your prayer."

"I'm not sure I've quit praying yet."

Noah grunted, fixing his gaze ahead at the inky, rain-slashed darkness. "Don't quit. We're going to need every prayer. It's going to be a very long night."

❧

Melissa leaned her head against the window, the glass frigid against her skin. What an impossibly long night it had been. She hadn't slept a moment lying in bed listening to the storm. And all morning she'd battled her conscience, her broken heart, and her sense of betrayal.

Sarah bustled behind her, folding, sorting, stowing garments into luggage.

But Melissa could drum up no enthusiasm for packing. She could only focus on the emptiness in her heart, the pain of loss and disillusionment. Sleety snow pattered on the panes; the wind howled under the eaves. Her bedroom door opened, and she turned.

"Why aren't you packing? Your train leaves this evening." Mother lifted the lid of a steamer trunk and sifted through the contents.

Melissa returned her gaze to the windows. Another gust slammed the house, sending snow swirling against the panes. Waves crashed on the rocky shore, flinging spume high in an icy veil. She closed her eyes, and the *Bethany* swam into her vision, tossed and helpless before towering seas. Had they reached a safe harbor? Anxiety tightened her chest. "Is there any word from the harbor on how the ships are faring in the storm?"

Mother gave a vinegary sound. "I've not inquired. Anyone foolhardy enough to leave port in the teeth of a storm deserves what he gets."

"But, Mother"—Melissa turned, eyes flying open—"the ships that left port yesterday afternoon left in fine weather. They couldn't know this would blow up." She waved toward the windows.

"Well, it's no business of ours. Get your belongings packed. Your father agrees that Aunt Persephone's is the best place for you. He's terribly upset about your broken engagement. I am, too. You've behaved very badly, and we're the ones who must bear the brunt of the embarrassment."

Melissa bit back all the words she wanted to say, all the protests about how she was the one wronged, how she wasn't some parcel to be mailed away at their convenience. It wouldn't matter now anyway.

Light flashed in the gray gloom outside. Thunder boomed, rattling the panes.

She pressed a hand to her throat. A chill raced up her arms. Any northerner knew thunderclaps during a snow only came during the most intense winter storms. Was Jonathan out on that raging lake, perhaps fighting for his life? "Sarah, please ask one of the footmen to go to the harbor and find out if there is any word of the *Bethany*." Melissa ignored her mother's gasp. "Tell him to ask the harbormaster and at Kennebrae Shipping if need be."

The lid of the steamer trunk slammed shut. "Melissa Brooke, I'll not have you asking after Jonathan Kennebrae like some heartbroken waif. People will think you're regretting your rash actions. How desperate do you think you'll look?"

Melissa set her jaw and turned toward her mother. "Right now I don't care how I look. Jonathan and Noah sailed out yesterday afternoon. I need to know if there is any word of them before I leave for San Francisco."

Mother huffed and frowned then shrugged. "There's nothing I can do with you. I give up." She lifted her hands and let them drop to her sides. "Your reputation's ruined as it is. Go ahead and traipse down to the docks yourself. Snivel after the Kennebraes like some needy puppy."

Melissa rolled her eyes at her mother's dramatics.

Poor Sarah had frozen, not knowing which mistress to obey.

"Please, Sarah, send word for the automobile to be brought around. Mother is right. It would be best if I went myself."

twenty-two

Jonathan rolled his shoulders to ease his tense muscles. Cold, cramped, and exhausted, he stood at his brother's side on the bridge.

The bilge pumps chugged, trying to stay ahead of the incoming water. The wind continued to roar, driving the waves to ever-mounting heights. The ship rolled and shuddered while the helmsman fought the wheel. The *Galilee* hung behind on the towrope, slewing and bucking but holding her own.

The *Bethany* listed about two feet down on the starboard side. Noah ordered several deckhands into the hold to shift iron ore to the port side with shovels.

Jonathan didn't envy them trying to stay upright and move the filthy reddish gray ore in the tight confines of the cargo compartments.

The Two Harbors light gave Jonathan some hope they were nearing safety.

But rather than turn broadside to the waves again to enter Agate Bay, Noah ordered the helmsman to sail on to Duluth. "I won't risk the sharp turn into Two Harbors. Duluth Harbor gives us a straight run to shelter." Noah answered the helmsman's unspoken question.

Though a seaman had nailed an oilskin over the broken window, the pilothouse remained cold.

"It will feel good to get some solid ground under my feet." Jonathan stomped his feet and blew into his gloved hands. "And I'm glad for the daylight, weak as it is in this storm. Last night was terrible."

Noah spared him a glance and a slight smile. "Good thing you're not prone to seasickness."

"You've done a marvelous job, little brother. I don't know

of any captain who could've done better. We're almost home free."

Noah shook his head, his eyes on the waves crashing over the bow. He leaned in and lowered his voice. "We're not there yet. The list hasn't improved, which means we're taking on water faster than I thought. And we've got to make the harbor entrance in the worst seas I've ever seen. That opening is narrow and protected by two cement piers. We'll be lucky to get in without some hull damage."

Jonathan took in his brother's clouded eyes, his rigid expression. Responsibility for the ship, the consort barge, and the crews of both lay heavily on Noah.

"Why don't you go below for a while? Nothing's changing up here. You need some rest."

Noah shook his head. "I'll rest later. I belong here."

The watch changed. A new helmsman took the wheel. Two more hours of struggling through the storm.

Through the gloom, the green light of the south breakwater lighthouse of Duluth Harbor cast an eerie shaft toward them. Jonathan rubbed his gritty eyes, straining through the lashing water to make sure he wasn't hallucinating.

A cheer went up from the crew. Safety lay ahead.

❧

"Miss, I'm a little busy. You'll have to wait." The harbormaster pushed past Melissa. "Joe, get that tug brought around to where it can be of some use. We've already got one ship grounded on the shore. We don't need another one."

"I just want to know if there's been any word at all." She hurried after him, the wind tugging at her skirt and coat, pulling at her hair.

"Miss, go check at the shipping office." He all but thrust her away in his haste.

Melissa fought through the crowd gathered on the pier. What were so many people doing out here in this weather? The temperature couldn't be much above zero, yet folks were milling about.

The talk was all of the *R. W. England*, a brand-new steamer, beached up the shore, its hull cracked open to the surf. At least the crew had been rescued.

She could make out the hulks of a dozen ships at anchor in the harbor basin and several more outside the safety of the breakwaters straining at their anchor chains. Fog and fitful snow tussled around her. She needed to get to the Kennebrae offices. The top of the building loomed three blocks west and only one block from the lake. She wouldn't bother going back to the automobile. Getting down to the harbor had been difficult enough.

She wrapped her coat tighter about herself and ducked her head against the cutting wind. Her lungs ached with cold, and her feet were numb. If only she'd thought to ask someone— Sarah maybe—to come with her, she might not feel so alone, so anxious.

Her throat tightened when she reached the steps of the Kennebrae Building. For a moment she stood on the marble stairs, battling her pride and heartache against her need for news of the *Bethany*. Another gust ripped between the buildings, almost pushing her over.

The heavy door yielded under her hand, and the gale blew her inside. The calm warmth of the lobby pressed in on her freezing face. She panted, trying to catch her breath.

A bespectacled man behind a desk rose and came toward her. "May I help you, miss?"

For a moment she couldn't speak. Then she bolstered her courage and lifted her chin. "I'd like to see Mr. Abraham Kennebrae. Is he in?"

"I'll check. May I tell him who is calling?"

"Tell him Melissa Brooke."

She almost laughed at the man's startled glance. He must've read the papers. "Wait here." He scurried toward the stairs, stopping at the landing and peering over the banister at her.

She caught sight of herself in the mirror on the far wall. Her hair flew about her face in medusa-like swirls, her cheeks

146 The Bartered Bride

raw and red. She hadn't bothered with a hat when she left the house, but now she wished she had. She scrabbled for a handkerchief.

"This way, Miss Brooke." He led her up two flights of stairs.

A shaft of pain sliced her heart as they passed Jonathan's closed office door, but she kept her eyes forward, her hands at her sides.

The man kept darting looks at her over his shoulder, as if expecting her to burst into hysterics. They reached the end of the hallway where he rapped twice on a door and opened it. "Miss Brooke, sir."

Melissa entered, and the man closed the door behind her.

Mr. Kennebrae sat in his wheelchair at the corner windows looking down on the harbor.

She took off her gloves and smoothed back her hair.

"Come here, child." His voice sounded frail and raspy.

She walked toward him, tucking her gloves into her pocket. A fire burned in the fireplace, casting a glow in the storm-darkened room. When she reached him, he held out his hand to her.

His skin was papery white, wrinkled, and spotted. His breath scraped in his throat. He seemed to have shrunk since the last time she'd seen him, resplendent in evening dress at the ball. Then he had been a titan of business, the head of a proud family. Now he looked like an old man broken by sorrow. His state of decline alarmed her. Had he gotten bad news?

She forced the words past the lump in her throat. "Mr. Kennebrae, I came to ask if there was any word of the *Bethany*. I know she put out yesterday."

He looked up at her with rheumy eyes. "I'm sorry, lass. More sorry than I can say. There's been no word of her." Coughs wracked him, his thin shoulders shaking under the effort of drawing breath. "Bronchitis. It comes on with the cold weather."

"Can I get you something?"

He shook his head. "Just sit with me. I have things to tell you."

She tugged off her coat and draped it on the end of his desk. Several chairs stood at attention down the side of a conference table, so she took the end one and placed it beside him where she could see his profile.

"I feel terrible about what's happened. I opened my mouth when I shouldn't have." He never took his eyes off the waves. "You see, Jonathan told me you thought he'd spilled the secret about your suffrage activities to me. But, my dear, Jonathan never said a word. In fact, I didn't know *he* knew. When I first hit on the idea of you two marrying, I had you thoroughly checked out. Didn't want any unpleasant surprises. I knew all about the meetings, and I knew when they were moved to this building. Dawkins, night guard here for years—trust him implicitly—he told me everything."

She gasped.

He took her hand, squeezing it. "Now, now, don't be upset. I knew long ago about your work with the illiterate women of the city and about your desire to see women given the right to vote. I know about your schooling, your dislike of seafood, and even your habit of biting your nails when you're worried." He took his gaze from the windows and inclined his head at her.

She took her thumbnail out of her mouth and dropped her hand to her lap, feeling heat surge up her neck.

"My dear, Jonathan didn't betray you in any way. He is as innocent in all this as you are. He knew nothing of my financial difficulties before he asked you to marry him. I deliberately kept it from him until afterwards."

Melissa swallowed hard, guilt at her accusations pressing against her chest.

"My grandson has a fearful temper. Gets it from me. We had quite a donnybrook when he found out. Don't blame Jonathan. The fault lies with me. I'll admit your mother and I jumped the gun a little with the announcement, but Jonathan proposed to you properly because he fell in love with you."

For a frozen moment Melissa was afraid to hope. Could he

be telling her the truth? She wanted to believe him, wanted to with an intensity she'd never known. Reality deflated her hopes. She'd accused Jonathan of trying to marry her for money. She'd flung awful words at him, thrown his love back in his face. He might have loved her once but no more, not after what she'd done.

Mr. Kennebrae gave a rueful laugh. "You want to know the irony of it all?" He lifted some papers from his lap. "At the end of the last century, I took some property in Montana as payment for a debt. It's been sitting there, a chunk of mountain outside a little town called Butte. I got word today that the country's richest copper strike has been found out there. This is a telegram from William Rockefeller. His company, Amalgamated Copper, is offering me a scandalous amount for that patch of land. Enough to take care of all my debts and then some."

She blinked back tears. Poor old man. Trying so hard to make things work, when if he'd just trusted God to work out His plan, everything would've been fine.

Sound familiar?

Melissa frowned. Her conscience prodded her. She hadn't trusted God. She hadn't trusted anyone. And when things didn't work out the way she planned, she assumed it was God who had erred.

Oh, Lord, I'm sorry. Please forgive me. Help me to trust You with everything in my life. And, Lord, please watch over the Bethany. *Keep them safe. I need to apologize to Jonathan. You know how much I love him. Please, Lord, give me a chance to make things right. I'll try to understand if he can't forgive me, but give me the courage. . .and the chance. . .to make things right.*

Tears crept down the old man's cheeks.

She clung to his hand, praying for him, for both of them, and for his grandsons.

After a while he stirred. "I don't suppose you'd know, but Jonathan and I had a fight before he left. I said some harsh things to him that I'm ashamed of now. He's left the family business for good. He's going to work in Erie, Pennsylvania. A fellow called Fox has hired him to oversee his shipping line." His voice cracked. "I don't blame him."

Going to work in Pennsylvania? Not coming back to Duluth? Her shoulders sagged. "We're more alike than you'd think, Mr. Kennebrae. We both broke his heart."

A knock sounded at the door. The man from the front desk stuck his head inside. "Sir, the *Bethany* has been sighted heading toward the harbor."

Melissa blinked, sending tears, this time of thankfulness, down her cheeks. "I'm going down to the harbor. I have to be there when he comes in." Melissa straightened, wiping her cheeks with the backs of her hands, unable to stop her smiling.

"I couldn't imagine a better homecoming, my dear."

"He may not want to speak to me." She shrugged into her coat and buttoned it up the front.

"Then you'll have to make him listen. Kennebraes are stubborn, but when we love, it's forever. He still loves you. He just needs to be reminded."

twenty-three

Waves pounded the *Bethany*, each one seeming larger than the last. Snow buffeted the pilothouse, scouring the windows, fine as salt.

Jonathan rubbed his sleeve on the window, swiping away condensation. Fog and snow impeded his vision so he couldn't make out individual houses and buildings of Duluth. Only the hulking shape of land and the white spray of the surf against the rocky shore flitted through swirling flakes.

Farther south, toward the harbor, watery lights shone fitfully, hazed by precipitation. Jonathan hunched his shoulders and crossed his arms, trying to hold some warmth in.

"We cannot make it into the harbor with the *Galilee* in tow. The canal's too narrow. We'll be lucky to make it in ourselves." Noah ran his hand down his face and beard.

His first mate lurched against the wall as the *Bethany* took another brutal wave. "Can't we drop the anchors here and try to ride it out?"

"No, we're taking on too much water. The pumps are falling behind. We've got to make the harbor. The hatches amidships are leaking too much." Noah straightened his shoulders. "Signal the *Galilee* we're dropping the towlines. She'll have to set her anchors and ride out the storm as best she can. If we try to take her through the canal, she'll be battered to death on the piers."

The first mate ducked out the door, struggling to close it behind him in the wind.

Jonathan went into the chart room to look aft. The *Galilee* bucked along at the end of the steel hawser. Men clung to the rail, working their way back toward the towline, their feet slipping on the icy deck, buffeted with every step.

Light flashes and the barest glimpse of the hulk of the consort barge. Jonathan strained to see through the storm. Signal lamps, Morse code.

The door clanged open. Icy air blasted them as the first mate ducked inside the wheelhouse. "*Galilee* says she'll drop anchor, Captain."

"Very well. Release the towline."

The *Bethany* seemed to rise in the water a bit and surge forward. The towline to their consort had been dropped.

"All ahead full." Noah dialed the chadburn. He then returned to his high captain's chair. Jonathan stood at his shoulder, hanging onto the back of the chair. A wave burst over the ship, momentarily blinding them with spray.

"Left ten degrees. Line up off the south pier light."

Jonathan watched the channel between the piers grow larger as they approached. Steerage had to be corrected every few seconds, it seemed, as the storm buffeted them. Snow wreathed the steel framework of the transporter bridge across the far end of the canal. If they could just make it under the bridge, they'd be safe in the harbor. A fleet of tugs would assist them in getting to the docks.

The *Bethany* carried fifty feet of beam. The canal was one hundred thirty feet wide. Steel and concrete piers guarded the entrance through Minnesota Point into the harbor. Almost there.

The nose of the ship entered the canal fairly straight. Jonathan exhaled and lifted his hand to clap Noah on the shoulder. Before his hand descended, the boat's stern lifted high on a rogue wave shoving the vessel forward, throwing Noah against the front wall of the wheelhouse. The helmsman crashed into him, the wheel spinning wildly.

Jonathan's feet left the deck, and he tumbled over the bolted-down chair into the wheel. His shoulder slammed one of the handles, breaking it off.

The bow gave a sickening crunch as it hit the bottom of the canal and bobbed up again.

Arms and legs scrambled. Men yelled.

Jonathan's shoulder burned, but he pushed himself off the floor.

"The captain's hurt!" The helmsman grabbed for the spinning wheel. "Look out!"

Another monstrous wave hit them, crashing them into the north pier.

Jonathan, staggering to his feet to go to Noah, was hurled into his brother.

"What do I do?" The helmsman ducked as shards from the breaking windows exploded into the tiny space.

Jonathan threw himself over Noah's defenseless form, trying to protect him from the flying glass.

Water poured into the broken window followed by a gust of icy air.

Noah groaned.

Jonathan scrambled to his feet.

Noah propped himself up on his palms, water swilling about his hands and knees. Blood dripped from a gash on his head.

Jonathan swiped the water from his eyes and tried to locate the pier wall through the window.

The *Bethany* careened crazily, her stern yawing and dragging them outside the canal walls. The engine throbbed at full throttle, but the wheel spun helplessly in the helmsman's hands. "I've got nothing. It's like the rudder's gone."

"Noah, are you all right?" Jonathan grabbed the arm of the captain's chair to keep from being tossed down again.

They were broadside to the merciless waves and being shoved toward the shore. The keel ground on the rocks of the lake bed. With a final thudding jolt, forty-eight hundred tons came to a stop, foundered on a shoal more than one hundred yards offshore.

❧

Melissa shouldered her way through the crowd, hoping to make it to pier side in time to see the *Bethany* come in.

Snow spiraled around her on a cutting wind, the air damp with the spray of the waves thrashing the rock-strewn shore perpendicular to the jutting pier. Perhaps she should've gone by automobile around the harbor to the docks and met the ship there.

"She's in trouble. Look!" A man shouted just ahead of her, pointing toward the lake. "She's going to capsize!"

Melissa snaked between the onlookers, not stopping until she reached the pier wall. She scraped her wet hair out of her eyes and leaned out to catch a glimpse of the *Bethany*.

A mighty wave picked up the back end of the ship and thrust her nose downward. The scrunch as her bow hit the bottom of the canal ricocheted off the pier walls. Another storm surge swatted at her, cracking her against the north pier. The shock to the ship made it shudder.

Melissa screamed, her voice drowned out in the shriek of the storm. She gripped rough concrete, her body buffeted by onlookers trying to see better. The crowd forced her to fall back, pushing, running toward the shoreline on her left. The only thing she could see above the crowd was the top of the steamer's smokestack.

She left the sidewalk and struggled over the icy boulders, feet slipping, numb hands spread wide for balance, grasping, climbing.

"She's hit the shoal! Launch the lifeboats! Look! She's tearing apart!" Men shouted all around Melissa.

She wiped water from her face.

The *Bethany* sat abeam of the shore, barely a hundred yards away, waves pounding her amidships, spilling over the deck. Her midsection strained, then a crack appeared, wider with each slam of water.

"She's down in the stern. Look, you can see men on the deck!"

The stern settled lower in the water. A huge hiss and billow of steam jetted into the air.

"Her boiler room's flooded. They're powerless now."

The strength drained from Melissa's limbs. The wind

snarled her hair, tangling it and throwing it across her face like a wet veil. No steam. No power. No heat.

"Miss! Miss Brooke!" Hands grabbed her. She swung around to look up into the face of McKay, the Kennebrae butler. His ashen face stood out in the gloom. "This way, Miss Brooke."

"How did you get here?" She'd had too many shocks to think clearly. Numbness leeched all drive and energy from her.

"I came to fetch Mr. Kennebrae from his office. We saw the crowds from the window. He wanted me to come after you and see that you came to no harm."

"Oh, McKay, they hit the pier."

"I know, miss." His strong hands helped her back up the rocks to the street.

"She's sinking. Did you see her? She's broken in two."

"Yes, miss. This way. Come back from the shore. It's too dangerous to be out there."

"Where are we going?"

"To the office. You need to get warmed and dry. The boys will be brought there when the lifesavers get them off the ship."

She followed him like an obedient child, too stunned to do anything else.

❧

Jonathan patted Noah's face. "Hey, wake up, little brother. We need you here."

Noah groaned, eyes cloudy and unfocused. "Wha' 'appen'd?"

"We're aground outside the harbor just offshore."

"My ship." Noah put his hand to his forehead. A nasty gash over his right eye bled freely.

"She's in bad shape, Noah." Jonathan squeezed his brother's shoulder. "She's down in the stern, no steam, and she's got a bad break in the middle. We're almost completely separated from the bow."

"Casualties?"

Jonathan was relieved to see sense coming back into Noah's eyes. "Some cuts and bruises, yours by far the worst. The first mate says there are men in the bow section of the ship. We don't know their status."

"Help me up."

Jonathan stood and assisted Noah to his feet.

Cold air whistled through the pilothouse from every broken window. The ship rocked hard to port with each wave pounding over her spar deck. Crew members crowded into the wheelhouse and chart room.

Jonathan tried to look away from their shocked, scared faces. He battled down his own fear, beating it back until he could think clearly.

Noah clamped a handkerchief to his bleeding head. "We're hard against the shoal, too heavy to be pushed over it. We'll be pounded apart against it." He stopped, closing his eyes and holding his chest.

"Noah?" Jonathan touched his brother's arm. *Please, God, don't take Noah.*

"I'm all right. Just knocked my ribs a bit." Noah addressed the first mate. "Light the lamp, and signal the bow. Find out what's happening up there."

"Someone's headed this way from the bow, Captain."

The men in the pilothouse surged to the windows. Four sailors picked their way across the flooded deck, clinging to the icy wire railing. Their feet slipped, bodies blown and shoved by the wind. Those in the pilothouse could do nothing but watch their perilous journey. A roll of black water broke over the men on deck, and when it receded, there were only three.

Jonathan gripped the window frame. Just like that, the lake had swallowed a victim. Jonathan willed the remaining men to be careful, his mind racing in prayer.

They reached the crack in the ship. Jonathan held his breath as first one, then another leaped the gap. A wave crashed into the ship, sending water thrusting upward into the breach like a geyser. The third man hung back, both hands tight on the rail.

The first two motioned for him to follow, but he stood still, shaking his head. Finally he turned back the way he had come. The two who remained on the deck crept forward until they reached the pilothouse.

"Captain, the ship's yawl was ripped away in the collision. There's nine men in the bow. We lost Cummings over the rail. Nobody who's left is hurt bad, just cold and scared."

Noah nodded, grim and pale.

Jonathan's heart thudded against his chest, and he had to force himself not to give in to fear.

One crewman, who couldn't be more than seventeen, pointed through the port windows. "I see the lifesavers' boat."

The white boat looked small against the angry waves. Lake Superior slapped at it, racing toward it in huge waves that thrust the bow of the little boat skyward, catapulting its occupants out like toys. Oars and sailors tumbled in the surf.

"They'll never reach us that way." Noah turned from the windows. "Bring every lantern you can find—and kerosene."

Men hurried out the starboard door.

Noah staggered.

"Sit down." Jonathan pushed him into the captain's chair and took the blood-soaked handkerchief. "Somebody get me something to bandage this cut with."

"Captain, they're signaling from the beach. They're going to try to shoot us a line with a Lyle gun and rig a breeches buoy to get us off."

Jonathan swallowed hard. As much as he desired to get off this ship, the thought of dangling like a piece of laundry from a rope over the churning water held little appeal. He dabbed at his brother's cut with the edge of the handkerchief.

"Take two more men, and see about securing that line when it comes." Noah swatted at Jonathan's ministrations. "Stop fussing. We've got to get off this ship."

❧

Jonathan put his weight into opening the port-side door. The list of the ship and the battering had bent the metal frame and bowed the steel door. Though he waited for the report of the Lyle gun, the sound couldn't reach them over the roar of the storm. Like a striking snake, a rope shot out of the fog.

Men on the deck below grappled with the line shot from the shore, making it fast to the ship.

"Won't be long now, Noah. They've got the line." Relief loosened Jonathan's jaw.

Noah pushed himself up. "Get the crew lined up. Youngest crewmen first then the officers. Jonathan, you go with the officers."

"I'll wait and go after you."

Noah's eyes hardened. "You'll do as you're told aboard my ship. The captain goes last."

They stepped outside into the swirling snow. The wind sucked Jonathan's breath from his lungs. Rigging aft of the pilothouse clanged. With every buffet the ship groaned and creaked in agony.

The breeches buoy swung out toward them, pitched by the waves. The cook's boy stepped to the rail, his face stoic but his eyes wide with fear. How old was he? Twelve, thirteen at the most? He was in for a wild ride.

Hands, numb from the cold, fumbled with the straps, sliding them up his legs. The first mate hooked the apparatus to the line. "Hold on tight. You're going to get wet as you near the shore. The line dips, so if you get stuck, reach up and start pulling yourself along. Right?"

The boy nodded, pinched with cold.

Jonathan helped swing the boy onto the rail. He tried to smile, to encourage the child. "Ready?"

Something cracked, and the line went limp, zinging into the churning water below. The boy tottered on the rail, flailing his arms.

Jonathan grabbed at the child's legs. For a moment they hung over the rail, their balance tipping them toward the water. With a supreme effort Jonathan threw himself backward onto the deck. He lay there gasping for breath, snarled in the breeches buoy and the young sailor.

"It froze. The line's gone."

Lights flashed again from the shore. Jonathan untangled himself from the broken rope and buckles, defeat pressing his shoulders. They'd have to wait for a new line. The cook's boy sat propped against the wall, eyes closed, taking great gulps of air.

"What's your name, son?" Jonathan scooted over to him, his shoulder throbbing.

"Padraig, sir." He opened sky blue eyes. "But you can call me Paddy." His brogue was as thick as his curly mop of dark hair. "Thank you, sir. I thought I was going swimming that time."

"Me, too."

The first mate turned from the rail. "They say they can't do anything more until the storm blows out. We're trapped here."

"Let's get inside the wheelhouse. It's going to be a long, cold night." Noah stood by the open door, waiting as a captain should, to be the last one inside.

twenty-four

Melissa sat before the fire in the Kennebrae offices, sipping the tea McKay brought her. Her damp skirts steamed in the warmth.

Mr. Kennebrae sat by the window, his eyes never leaving the ship stranded in the lake.

"Do you think God's punishing me?" His breath wheezed. "Taking my grandsons from me because I've been so negligent of Him?"

She swallowed her tea, the heat sliding down her throat, warming her from within. "I don't think God is as petty as we are, Mr. Kennebrae. He doesn't play tit-for-tat school-yard games. Everything He does is for our good and according to the purpose He's mapped out in our lives. Even when—or especially when—it isn't something that we would've chosen for ourselves."

"How do you know? You're so young."

She set her cup down and went to stand beside him at the windows. "Because the Bible says so. There's one verse I flung at God when I thought He'd abandoned me and was doing things to deliberately hurt me. But I was wrong. I know now it is true. There is nothing that happens that is outside the will of God. He doesn't follow us with a broom and dustpan, picking up the broken pieces of His plan that we smash, trying to put them back together somehow. And He doesn't shoot down lightning bolts of retribution on His children when they fall. He lifts us up, brushes us off, and forgives us."

"What verse?"

She smiled, in spite of her worry over Jonathan. "It's from Jeremiah. Chapter twenty-nine, verse eleven. 'For I know the thoughts that I think toward you, saith the Lord, thoughts of peace, and not of evil, to give you an expected end.'"

He sat silent for a moment. "So God knows our end."

She nodded. "He not only knows it, but He's planned it out ahead of time and knows it is good and not evil."

Abraham took her hand in his. "Thank you for comforting an old man in his distress. I can see what drew Jonathan to you. You are a treasure. When he gets back here, I'll do everything I can to see that you two are reconciled."

She withdrew her hand with a sad smile. "No, Mr. Kennebrae. I'll apologize to him, but that's all. If we are reconciled, it has to come from him. No more interference from well-meaning grandfathers." She sent him a pointed look. "God has things under control, right?"

Abraham chuckled. "All right, my dear."

A knock at the door and McKay entered. "I'm afraid there's bad news, sir. The lifesavers are unable to reach the ship under current conditions. They must wait until the storm dies down."

Abraham sat up in his chair. "That could take all night. And with no steam aboard ship, how will they keep warm?"

Melissa sagged against the windowsill. All night? *Oh, Lord, help me to hang on to the truth of Your Word. I know You are in control. Please, help them to survive. Please bring Jonathan and Noah back to us.*

She stood and gathered up her coat.

"Where are you going, young lady?"

"I'm going to the shore. I can't stay here in warmth and luxury when they are suffering so. I'm going to stand vigil and pray."

"I'll go with you. McKay, get my coat."

Melissa put her hand on his shoulder. "No, Abraham." He started—whether at her tone or at her use of his first name, she didn't know. "You're staying here. The weather's too raw. And there's your bronchitis to consider."

He sagged back. "Very well but, McKay, get her some proper outerwear and light a bonfire on the beach. If she starts to flag, haul her back here. I'll be in this room watching until my grandsons are rescued."

She bent and kissed him on the cheek. "Pray, Abraham."

❧

Aboard the *Bethany*, fifteen men huddled in the wheelhouse. Only three lamps had survived the wreck intact. They hung from hooks on the ceiling, rocking and swinging with the movement of the boat.

Jonathan anchored a piece of canvas to the window frame, trying to cover the gaping hole. The ship rolled and shuddered, slammed against the shoal by another frigid blast.

"Finish nailing that oilskin, and find something to brace that starboard door." Noah's voice sounded weaker by the minute. How bad were his injuries?

Jonathan spoke through lips stiffened by the cold. "Sit down, Noah, before you fall down."

"No, nobody sits. And nobody sleeps."

The men grumbled, scowling.

"That's an order. If you sit down, you'll fall asleep. If you fall asleep in this cold, you'll freeze to death. Understand?" For a moment light gleamed in Noah's eyes, the light of challenge and authority. The crew must've recognized that look, for they all nodded assent.

"Aye, Captain, no sleeping."

Paddy kept close to Jonathan's side. With no food and no water, some of the men resorted to breaking off icicles and sucking on them. Jonathan, already so cold, couldn't bring himself to do this. At least not yet.

"Is there any word from the men in the bow?" Noah wedged himself next to Jonathan in the corner of the tiny room.

Jonathan kept his voice low. "None since dark."

Concern laced Noah's voice. "Are there any lamps lit up there?"

"No, I didn't see any."

"Where there's light, there's hope, you know?"

They both looked at the three lamps throwing yellow light

on the crowded room. How long would their only heat source, these three tiny flames, last?

a

"Miss, stand back. They're going to light it." McKay tugged on Melissa's arm.

She stepped back on the street.

A burly stevedore stuck his torch into the kerosene-soaked pile of crating and firewood. Flames shot out, licking upward, throwing light and heat toward the ring of onlookers. Dockworkers, shopkeepers, housewives, and sailors crowded the pier and the streets of Minnesota Point. Several more bonfires burst up along the expanse of shoreline.

"There must be thousands of people out here keeping vigil." McKay led her to the pier wall. "And look, there's some light coming from the wheelhouse. Why, I bet those boys are in there watching us, taking heart knowing they aren't alone and haven't been forgotten."

Melissa wiped her cheeks, grateful for the heavy gloves McKay had found for her. And in the whipping snow and wind, grateful to have her hair confined under the hood of the heavy cloak he'd procured. The man was a marvel of efficiency. She almost smiled when he handed her a cup of steaming coffee. Was there anything he couldn't do?

Ladies from the church milled through the crowd, pouring coffee and offering food.

Pastor Gardner, muffled to the eyes in a buffalo coat and muskrat hat, clutched his Bible to his chest and prayed.

Melissa kept her vigil, adding her prayers to the hundreds being said on behalf of the men stranded on the ship. She spoke only to McKay and then only when he asked her a direct question. All her thoughts centered on Jonathan. She loved him. Even if he couldn't forgive her for what she'd done to him, she wanted him to know how sorry she was and how much he meant to her. She kept her eyes on the lights in the wheelhouse.

Sometime near 3:00 a.m., someone began to sing.

"Brightly beams our Father's mercy
From His lighthouse evermore,
But to us He gives the keeping
Of the lights along the shore.

Let the lower lights be burning!
Send a gleam across the wave!
Some poor fainting, struggling seaman
You may rescue, you may save."

Melissa's eyes filled with tears. A few voices joined the lone singer. She added her own, singing the familiar hymn with new understanding of the beautiful picture.

"Eager eyes are watching, longing,
For the lights along the shore."

More in the crowd began to sing, sending their message of hope across the waves to the sailors of the *Bethany*.

"Trim your feeble lamp, my brother,
Some poor sailor tempest tossed,
Trying now to make the harbor,
In the darkness may be lost."

❧

Jonathan shook his head to clear his fuzzy brain. The unending buffeting made thinking difficult. He couldn't feel his hands or feet anymore, not even when he stomped or beat his arms across his chest. The sleeves of his coat crackled with ice.

The elation he'd felt at seeing the bonfires springing up along the shore had worn off. What he wouldn't give to be standing next to one of them now. He let his mind drift to the one topic he'd been avoiding for hours.

Melissa.

Lord, I've been a knot-headed fool about her from the moment

I first heard her name. Why is it that love makes a man act so stupidly? I've ignored Your Spirit's promptings, and I've tried to handle everything my own way. I've lost my temper, and I've lost my head.

"What are you mumbling about?" Noah stifled a yawn and recrossed his arms, tucking his fingers under his armpits.

"I'm telling God what a fool I've been over Melissa."

Noah grunted. "Is He agreeing with you?"

Jonathan ignored that dig. "Truth is, I prayed for weeks this Bible verse, but I think I was praying it all wrong."

"What verse?"

"Proverbs 21:1. 'The king's heart is in the hand of the Lord, as the rivers of water: he turneth it whithersoever he will.' I prayed that over Grandfather a hundred times, wanting God to change his heart about this marriage. And I prayed it over Melissa, wanting God to change her heart toward me these last few days. The only one I didn't pray it over was me."

"And God took your heart and changed it a bunch, didn't He?" Noah's words came out clipped, his jaw clamped.

"He sure did. He let me fall in love with Melissa. He opened my eyes to the plight of the immigrants we hire, particularly their wives. And the plight of women in this country who don't get a voice in its leadership." Jonathan broke off, shifting his weight, rubbing his hands on his upper arms.

"But most of all, He changed how I felt about myself and my possessions. I was and still am willing to give up Kennebrae Shipping if it means I could have Melissa forgive me. Kennebrae Shipping isn't my life. Serving God is my life. And my life would be so much better with Melissa at my side." Jonathan's teeth chattered, and he bit down hard to still them.

"That's a heap of change."

"Facing death by shipwreck will cause you to evaluate a few things."

"So God shipwrecked us so He could drill some sense

into that anvil-hard head of yours? You're like Jonah." Noah's mouth barely moved. "Remind me when we get off of here to slug you a good one."

"The first thing I'm going to do when I get onshore is go to Castlebrooke and make Melissa listen to me, even if I have to break down her door."

What was that? He cocked an ear. The wind, gusting for hours, seemed to die down a bit. Was that singing?

"I must be more tired than I thought." Jonathan put his arm around little Paddy, rocking with tiredness, and briskly rubbed the lad's arms to warm him. "I could've sworn I heard Grandmother's favorite hymn. Remember how she used to sing 'Let the Lower Lights Be Burning' every night it stormed on Lake Superior?"

twenty-five

Dawn broke, if so gray and overcast an event could be called dawn. The storm relented at last, snarling and spitting in retreat up the north shore. The waves lost their fury, subsiding slowly but steadily.

Melissa's pulse beat in her throat as the lifesavers put their boat into the water once more. With coordinated strokes, they bent the oars, taking the waves and rising over them, heading out to the *Bethany*. Melissa couldn't tell if the lights still burned in the wheelhouse.

A cheer went up when the door on the port side of the pilothouse opened and a dark-clad figure stepped out. Someone was alive!

"Please, God, let it be Jonathan." Contrition struck her. She wasn't the only woman on the beach who had a loved one on that ship. Other prayers for husbands and sons must be winging heavenward at that moment.

She tugged at her glove to bare her fingers so she could chew her thumbnail. Bad habits be hanged. She leaned against the concrete pier, straining to see.

"I have faith, my dear, that you'll see him soon."

She looked down to see Abraham Kennebrae at her elbow. Dawkins, the security guard from the Kennebrae Building, and McKay stood behind.

The butler winked at her then blew on his hands, shifting his weight. He'd not left her side all night, fetching her hot drinks, bringing a lap robe from the Kennebrae carriage to drape around her shoulders.

Abraham reached up and took her hand. "I made Dawkins bring me down. I couldn't stay up there anymore."

The white boat reached the *Bethany*, and several of the

166

lifesavers clambered aboard. It wouldn't be long now.

She bit her nail harder. Would he be alive? Would he forgive her?

❧

"I'm going forward with the lifesavers. Come if you want to, but as captain it's my duty." Noah shrugged off Jonathan's hand and stepped out onto the rocking deck.

Jonathan blew out a sigh at the stubbornness of the Kennebraes and followed his brother toward the bow. His boots slipped and slid on the icy deck, but at least the waves weren't crashing over him, threatening to sweep him over the rail.

The crack in the hull was narrowest on the starboard side and a matter of a quick jump to cross. Iron ore eddied red swirls just under the surface where the hold lay open to the lake.

The scene in the bow was grim indeed. Nine sailors had roped themselves together, lashing themselves to the deck so as not to be swept overboard. All nine lay frozen to the ship, dead.

Noah seemed to crumple from within. He staggered, his face going pale.

Jonathan grabbed him to keep him from sliding to the deck.

"That's it. We're going now. No arguing." They maneuvered back to the stern of the ship and into the lifesavers' boat.

❧

Melissa insisted McKay stay with Abraham. If it was bad news, she wanted to hear it first and perhaps be able to tell Abraham gently. She picked her way down through the boulders to the shore.

Bits of flotsam and wreckage bumped against the rocks in the icy breeze. The lifesavers' boat scraped on the beach, loaded down with men. Bodies crowded around, blocking her view.

She pushed and wedged herself between the curious until she reached the front.

Strong hands lifted the survivors over the gunwale. They

were so bound in blankets and coats and mufflers that she couldn't recognize any of them.

A bearded face emerged from the boat. Noah! Alive!

Her heart thudded in her ears. She elbowed a man in the side and darted forward when he moved in surprise.

Dried blood decorated Noah's pale face. What had happened to him?

Then she looked past Noah's shoulder and into Jonathan's eyes. Her heart quit beating altogether, her breath gone. He was alive! Her mouth dropped open to speak, but no sound came out. She tried again.

He leaped from the boat, staggering as his boots hit the icy water. In two strides he wrapped her in his arms, covering her face with kisses, tunneling his fingers into her hair, dislodging her hood.

She kissed him back, cupping his cold cheeks in her hands, relishing being in his embrace. All misunderstanding, all the hurt and foolishness drained away.

He pulled back to look at her face, searching for something there. "I'm reading a lot into your being here, you know?"

"I know. Jonathan, there's something I need to say to you."

"Unless it's 'I love you,' it can wait."

"Jonathan, I love you."

"Melissa, I love you, too." He crushed her to him again, kissing her, filling up her cup of happiness until it overflowed into tears of joy.

When he released her, it was only to dig in his breast pocket. He withdrew her engagement ring and slipped it on her finger. "Right where it belongs, my love."

She wiped an icy tear from his cheek and nodded, too overcome for words.

epilogue

"You look lovely, my dear." Father leaned in and kissed Melissa's cheek. "Absolutely radiant."

Mother mopped her eyes. She'd cried all through the ceremony, though with happiness over Melissa's wedding to Jonathan or mourning over the fact that it wasn't the opulent festivities she'd originally planned, Melissa didn't know.

Jonathan lifted her hand, the one with the sapphire and diamond engagement ring and now the gold circlet he'd placed there only an hour before, and tucked it into his elbow. "Well, Mrs. Kennebrae."

She thrilled at both her new name and the depth of his voice brushing over her.

"Happy?"

"Deliriously." She squeezed his upper arm, leaning against him.

The reception at Castlebrooke was in full sail, guests laughing, music wafting from the piano.

"Mother's not sure how to react, but I'm glad we invited the suffragists and their families. And the Brittens. Peter and Wilson look like they're having a wonderful time. Thank you for thinking of it."

"It was the least I could do. Though Peter and Wilson won't need to act as your bodyguards any longer. No more late-night rambles to the harbor. From now on you hold your meetings in the parlor at Kennebrae House in a civilized manner. How about another dance?"

He looked at her so intently that a shiver raced up her spine. She smiled up at him and went into his arms like coming home.

He nuzzled her neck and whispered into her ear. "You look beautiful in that dress. Almost as beautiful as you looked standing on the shore in the wind and snow after a night's vigil in a storm."

She trembled, thinking of how close they'd come to losing each other forever. His grip tightened, and she knew he was thinking the same thing. "You're stuck with me now though. I heard you promise before God and all your friends."

"My bartered bride, you'll hear no complaints from me."

A Letter To Our Readers

Dear Reader:
In order that we might better contribute to your reading enjoyment, we would appreciate your taking a few minutes to respond to the following questions. We welcome your comments and read each form and letter we receive. When completed, please return to the following:

Fiction Editor
Heartsong Presents
PO Box 719
Uhrichsville, Ohio 44683

1. Did you enjoy reading *The Bartered Bride* by Erica Vetsch?
   ❑ Very much! I would like to see more books by this author!
   ❑ Moderately. I would have enjoyed it more if

   _____

   _____

   _____

2. Are you a member of **Heartsong Presents**? ❑ Yes ❑ No
   If no, where did you purchase this book? _____

   _____

3. How would you rate, on a scale from 1 (poor) to 5 (superior), the cover design? _____

4. On a scale from 1 (poor) to 10 (superior), please rate the following elements:

   ____ Heroine   ____ Plot
   ____ Hero   ____ Inspirational theme
   ____ Setting   ____ Secondary characters

5. These characters were special because? _____

_____

_____

6. How has this book inspired your life? _____

_____

_____

7. What settings would you like to see covered in future
   Heartsong Presents books? _____

_____

_____

8. What are some inspirational themes you would like to see
   treated in future books? _____

_____

_____

9. Would you be interested in reading other **Heartsong
   Presents** titles? ❏ Yes ❏ No

10. Please check your age range:
      ❏ Under 18   ❏ 18-24
      ❏ 25-34   ❏ 35-45
      ❏ 46-55   ❏ Over 55

Name _____

Occupation _____

Address _____

City, State, Zip _____

E-mail _____

THE BRIDE
BLUNDER

Presents